P
OUR TREES STILL GROW IN ...

Born in Kasauli, Himachal Pradesh, in 1934, Ruskin Bond grew up in Jamnagar (Gujarat), Dehra Dun and Shimla. His first novel, *Room on the Roof*, written when he was seventeen, received the John Llewllyn Rhys Memorial Prize in 1957. Since then he has written three hundred short stories, essays and novellas (including *Vagrants in the Valley* and *Flight of Pigeons*) and more than thirty books for children. He has also published two volumes of autobiography, *Scenes from a Writer's Life*, which describes his formative years growing up in Anglo-India, and *The Lamp is Lit*, a collection of essays and episodes from his journal. In 1992 he received the Sahitya Akademi award for English writing in India. He was awarded the Padma Shree in 1999.

Ruskin Bond lives with his adopted family in Mussoorie.

Our Trees Still Grow in Dehra

Stories

Ruskin Bond

PENGUIN BOOKS

Penguin Books India (P) Ltd., 11 Community Centre, Panchsheel Park, New Delhi 110017, India
Penguin Books Ltd., 80 Strand, London WC2R 0RL, UK
Penguin Group Inc., 375 Hudson Street, New York, NY 10014, USA
Penguin Books Australia Ltd., 250 Camberwell Road, Camberwell, Victoria 3124, Australia
Penguin Books Canada Ltd., 10 Alcorn Avenue, Suite 300, Toronto, Ontario M4V 3B2, Canada
Penguin Books (NZ) Ltd., Cnr Rosedale & Airborne Roads, Albany, Auckland, New Zealand
Penguin Books (South Africa) (Pty) Ltd., 24 Sturdee Avenue, Rosebank 2196, South Africa

First published by Penguin Books India 1991

Copyright © Ruskin Bond 1991

'Binya Passes By', 'From Small Beginnings' and 'Death of the Trees' are appearing here for the first time.

A *Flight of Pigeons* was made into the Hindi Film *Junoon* (directed by Shyam Benegal and produced by Shashi Kapoor).

All rights reserved

10 9 8

Typeset in New Baskerville by J. S. Enterprises, New Delhi

Printed at Pauls Press, New Delhi

Contents

For Prem and the family

*

As my stuff settles into shape, I am told (and sometimes myself discover, uneasily, but feel all right about it in calmer moments) it is mainly autobiographic and even egotistic after all—which I finally accept, and am contented so.

– Walt Whitman

Return to Dehra

So this is old Dehra of mangoes and lemons,
Where I grew beside the jackfruit tree
Planted by my father on the sunny side
Of the house since sold to Major-General Mehra.
The town's grown hard, none know me now or knew
My mother's laughter. Most men come home as strangers.
And yet, the trees my father planted here, these
Trees—old family trees—are growing still in Dehra.

Maplewood : An Introduction

It isn't many years since I left Maplewood, but I wouldn't be surprised to hear that the cottage has disappeared. Already, during my last months there, the trees were being cut and the new road was being blasted out of the mountain. It would pass just below the old cottage. There were (as far as I know) no plans to blow up the house; but it was already shaky and full of cracks, and a few tremors, such as those produced by passing trucks, drilling machines and bulldozers, would soon bring the cottage to the ground.

If it has gone, don't write and tell me: I'd rather not know.

When I moved in, it had been nestling there among the oaks for over seventy years. It had become a part of the forest. Birds nestled in the eaves; beetles burrowed in the woodwork; a jungle cat moved into the attic. Some denizens remained, even during my residence. And I was there—how long? Eight, nine years, I'm not sure; it was a timeless sort of place. Even the rent was paid only once a year, at a time of my choosing.

I first saw the cottage in late spring, when the surrounding forest was at its best—the oaks and maples in new leaf, the oak leaves a pale green, the maple leaves red and gold and bronze, turning to green as they matured; this is the Himalayan maple, quite different from the North American maple; only the winged seed-pods are similar, twisting and turning in the breeze as they fall to the ground, so that the Garhwalis call it the Butterfly Tree.

There was one very tall, very old maple above the cottage, and this was probably the tree that gave the house its name. A portion of it was blackened where it had been struck by lightning, but the rest of it lived on; a favourite haunt of woodpeckers: the ancient peeling bark seemed to harbour any number of tiny insects, and the woodpeckers would be tapping away all day, seeking to dislodge and devour their sweet, succulent prey.

A steep path ran down to the cottage. During heavy rain, it would become a watercourse and the earth would be washed away to leave it very stony and uneven. I first took this path to see Miss Mackenzie, an impoverished old lady who lived in two small rooms on the ground floor and who was acting on behalf of the owner. It was she who told me that the cottage was to let—provided she could remain in the portion downstairs.

Actually, the path ran straight across a landing and up to the front door of the first floor. It was the ground floor that was tucked away in the shadow of the hill; it was reached by a flight of steps, which also took the rush of water when the path was in flood.

Miss Mackenzie was eighty-six. I helped her up the steps and she opened the door for me. It led into an L-shaped room. There were two large windows, and when I pushed the first of these open, the forest seemed to rush upon me. The maples, oaks, rhododendrons, and an old walnut, moved closer, out of curiosity perhaps. A branch tapped against the window-panes, while from below, from the ravine, the deep-throated song of the whistling thrush burst upon me.

I told Miss Mackenzie I would take the place. She grew excited; it must have been lonely for her during the past several years, with most of the cottage lying empty, and only her old bearer and a mongrel dog for company. Her own house had been mortgaged to a moneylender. Her brothers and sisters were long dead. 'I'm the last Mackenzie in India,' she told me.

I told her I would move in soon: my books were still in Delhi. She gave me the keys and I left a cheque with her.

It was all done on an impulse—the decision to give up my job in Delhi, find a cheap house in a hill-station, and return to freelance writing. It was a dream I'd had for some time; lack of money had made it difficult to realize. But then, I knew that if I was going to wait for money to come, I might have to wait until I was old and grey and full of sleep. I was thirty-five—still young enough to take a few risks. If the dream was to become reality, this was the time to do something about it.

I don't know what led me to Maplewood; it was the first place I saw, and I did not bother to see any others. The location was far from being ideal. It faced east, and stood in the shadow of the Balahissar

Hill; so that while it received the early morning sun, it went without the evening sun. By three in the afternoon, the shadow of the hill crept over the cottage. This was all right in summer, but in winter it meant a cold, dark house.

There was no view of the snows and no view of the plains. In front stood Burnt Hill, or Pari Tibba (Hill of the Fairies), where apparently lightning played and struck more frequently than elsewhere. But the forest below the cottage seemed full of possibilities, and the windows opening on to it probably decided the issue. In my romantic frame of my mind, I was susceptible to magic casements opening wide.

I would make a window-seat and lie there on a summer's day, writing lyric poetry . . . .

But long before that could happen I was opening tins of sardines and sharing them with Miss Mackenzie. And then Prem came along. And there were others, like Binya.

I went away at times, but returned as soon as possible. Once you have lived with mountains, there is no escape. You belong to them.

Most of these stories (including those about my childhood) were written in Maplewood. So were many of the stories in my other two collections *The Night Train to Deoli* and *Time Stops at Shamli*. The old cottage was kind to a struggling young writer.

Mussoorie   Ruskin Bond
October, 1991

Escape from Java

It all happened within the space of a few days. The cassia tree had barely come into flower when the first bombs fell on Batavia (now called Jakarta) and the bright pink blossoms lay scattered over the wreckage in the streets.

News had reached us that Singapore had fallen to the Japanese. My father said: 'I expect it won't be long before they take Java. With the British defeated, how can the Dutch be expected to win!' He did not mean to be critical of the Dutch; he knew they did not have the backing of an Empire such as Britain then had. Singapore had been called the Gibraltar of the East. After its surrender there could only be retreat, a vast exodus of Europeans from South-East Asia.

It was World War II. What the Javanese thought about the war is now hard for me to say, because I was only nine at the time and knew very little of worldly matters. Most people knew they would be exchanging their Dutch rulers for Japanese rulers; but there were also many who spoke in terms of freedom for Java when the war was over.

Our neighbour, Mr Hartono, was one of those who looked ahead to a time when Java, Sumatra and the other islands would make up one independent nation. He was a college professor and spoke Dutch, Chinese, Javanese and a little English. His son, Sono, was about my age. He was the only boy I knew who could talk to me in English, and as a result we spent a lot of time together. Our favourite pastime was flying kites in the park.

The bombing soon put an end to kite flying. Air raid alerts sounded at all hours of the day and night, and although in the beginning most of the bombs fell near the docks, a couple of miles from where we lived, we had to stay indoors. If the planes sounded very near, we dived under beds or tables. I don't remember if there were any trenches. Probably there hadn't been time for trench digging, and now there was time only for digging graves. Events had moved all too swiftly, and everyone (except of course the Javanese) was anxious to get away from Java.

'When are you going?' asked Sono, as we sat on the veranda steps in a pause between air raids.

'I don't know,' I said. 'It all depends on my father.'

'My father says the Japs will be here in a week. And if you're still here then, they'll put you to work building a railway.'

'I wouldn't mind building a railway,' I said.

'But they won't give you enough to eat. Just rice with worms in it. And if you don't work properly, they'll shoot you.'

'They do that to soldiers,' I said. 'We're civilians.'

'They do it to civilians, too,' said Sono.

What were my father and I doing in Batavia, when our home had been first in India and then in Singapore? He worked for a firm dealing in rubber, and six months earlier he had been sent to Batavia to open a new office in partnership with a Dutch business house. Although I was so young, I accompanied my father almost everywhere. My mother left when I was very small, and my father had always looked after me. After the war was over he was going to take me to England.

'Are we going to win the war?' I asked.

'It doesn't look it from here,' he said.

No, it didn't look as though we were winning. Standing at the docks with my father, I watched the ships arrive from Singapore crowded with refugees—men, women and children, all living on the decks in the hot tropical sun; they looked pale and worn-out and worried. They were on their way to Colombo or Bombay. No one came ashore at Batavia. It wasn't British territory; it was Dutch, and everyone knew it wouldn't be Dutch for long.

'Aren't we going too?' I asked. 'Sono's father says the Japs will be here any day.'

'We've still got a few days,' said my father. He was a short, stocky man, who seldom got excited. If he was worried, he didn't show it. 'I've got to wind up a few business matters, and then we'll be off.'

'How will we go? There's no room for us on those ships.'

'There certainly isn't. But we'll find a way, lad, don't worry.'

I didn't worry. I had complete confidence in my father's ability to find a way out of difficulties. He used to say, 'Every problem has a solution hidden away somewhere, and if only you look hard enough you will find it.'

There were British soldiers in the streets but they did not make us feel much safer. They were just waiting for troop ships to come and take them away. No one, it seemed, was interested in defending Java, only in getting out as fast as possible.

Although the Dutch were unpopular with the Javanese people, there was no ill-feeling against individual Europeans. I could walk safely through the streets. Occasionally small boys in the crowded Chinese quarter would point at me and shout, *'Orang Balandi!'* (Dutchman!) but they did so in good humour, and I didn't know the language well enough to stop and explain that the English weren't Dutch. For them, all white people were the same, and understandably so.

My father's office was in the commercial area, along the canal banks. Our two-storied house, about a mile away, was an old building with a roof of red tiles and a broad balcony which had stone dragons at either end. There were flowers in the garden almost all the year round. If there was anything in Batavia more regular than the bombing, it was the rain, which came pattering down on the roof and on the banana fronds almost every afternoon. In the hot and steamy atmosphere of Java, the rain was always welcome.

There were no anti-aircraft guns in Batavia—at least we never heard any—and the Jap bombers came over at will, dropping their bombs by daylight. Sometimes bombs fell in the town. One day the building next to my father's office received a direct hit and tumbled into the river. A number of office workers were killed.

The schools closed, and Sono and I had nothing to do all day except sit in the house, playing darts or carrom, wrestling on the carpets, or playing the gramophone. We had records by

Gracie Fields, Harry Lauder, George Formby and Arthur Askey, all popular British artists of the early 1940s. One song by Arthur Askey made fun of Adolph Hitler, with the words, 'Adolph, we're gonna hang up your washing on the Siegfried Line, if the Siegfried Line's still there!' It made us feel quite cheerful to know that back in Britain people were confident of winning the war!

One day Sono said, 'The bombs are falling on Batavia, not in the countryside. Why don't we get cycles and ride out of town?'

I fell in with the idea at once. After the morning all-clear had sounded, we mounted our cycles and rode out of town. Mine was a hired cycle, but Sono's was his own. He'd had it since the age of five, and it was constantly in need of repairs. 'The soul has gone out of it,' he used to say.

Our fathers were at work; Sono's mother had gone out to do her shopping (during air raids she took shelter under the most convenient shop counter) and wouldn't be back for at least an hour. We expected to be back before lunch.

We were soon out of town, on a road that passed through rice fields, pineapple orchards and cinchona plantations. On our right lay dark green hills; on our left, groves of coconut palms and, beyond them, the sea. Men and women were working in the rice fields, knee-deep in mud, their broad-brimmed hats protecting them from the fierce sun. Here and there a buffalo wallowed in a pool of brown water, while a naked boy lay stretched out on the animal's broad back.

We took a bumpy track through the palms. They grew right down to the edge of the sea. Leaving our cycles on the shingle, we ran down a smooth, sandy beach and into the shallow water.

'Don't go too far in,' warned Sono. 'There may be sharks about.'

Wading in amongst the rocks, we searched for interesting shells, then sat down on a large rock and looked out to sea, where a sailing ship moved placidly on the crisp, blue waters. It was difficult to imagine that half the world was at war, and that Batavia, two or three miles away, was right in the middle of it.

On our way home we decided to take a short cut through the rice fields, but soon found that our tires got bogged down in the soft mud. This delayed our return; and to make things worse, we got the roads mixed up and reached an area of the town that seemed unfamiliar. We had barely entered the outskirts when the siren sounded, to be followed soon after by the drone of approaching aircraft.

'Should we get off our cycles and take shelter somewhere?' I called out.

'No, let's race home!' shouted Sono. 'The bombs won't fall here.'

But he was wrong. The planes flew in very low. Looking up for a moment, I saw the sun blotted out by the sinister shape of a Jap fighter-bomber. We pedalled furiously; but we had barely covered fifty yards when there was a terrific explosion on our right, behind some houses. The shock sent us spinning across the road. We were flung from our cycles. And the cycles, still propelled by the blast, crashed into a wall.

I felt a stinging sensation in my hands and legs, as though scores of little insects had bitten me. Tiny droplets of blood appeared here and there on my flesh. Sono was on all fours, crawling beside me, and I saw that he too had the same small scratches on his hands and forehead, made by tiny shards of flying glass.

We were quickly on our feet, and then we began running in the general direction of our homes. The twisted cycles lay forgotten on the road.

'Get off the street, you two!' shouted someone from a window; but we weren't going to stop running until we got home. And we ran faster than we'd ever run in our lives.

My father and Sono's parents were themselves running about the street, calling for us, when we came rushing around the corner and tumbled into their arms.

'Where have you been?'

'What happened to you?'

'How did you get those cuts?'

All superfluous questions; but before we could recover our breath and start explaining, we were bundled into our respective homes. My father washed my cuts and scratches, dabbed at my face and legs with iodine—ignoring my yelps—and then stuck plaster all over my face.

Sono and I had had a fright, and we did not venture far from the house again.

That night my father said: 'I think we'll be able to leave in a day or two.'

'Has another ship come in?'

'No.'

'Then how are we going? By plane?'

'Wait and see, lad. It isn't settled yet. But we won't be able to take much with us—just enough to fill a couple of travelling bags.'

'What about the stamp collection?' I asked.

My father's stamp collection was quite valuable and filled several volumes.

'I'm afraid we'll have to leave most of it behind,' he said. 'Perhaps Mr Hartono will keep it for me, and when the war is over— if it's over—we'll come back for it.'

'But we can take one or two albums with us, can't we?'

'I'll take one. There'll be room for one. Then if we're short of money in Bombay, we can sell the stamps.'

'Bombay? That's in India. I thought we were going back to England.'

'First we must go to India.'

The following morning I found Sono in the garden, patched up like me, and with one foot in a bandage. But he was as cheerful as ever and gave me his usual wide grin.

'We're leaving tomorrow,' I said.

The grin left his face.

'I will be sad when you go,' he said. 'But I will be glad too, because then you will be able to escape from the Japs.'

'After the war, I'll come back.'

'Yes, you must come back. And then, when we are big, we will go round the world together. I want to see England and America and Africa and India and Japan. I want to go everywhere.'

'We can't go everywhere.'

'Yes, we can. No one can stop us!'

We had to be up very early the next morning. Our bags had been packed late at night. We were taking a few clothes, some of my father's business papers, a pair of binoculars, one stamp album, and several bars of chocolate. I was pleased about the stamp album and the chocolates, but I had to give up several of my treasures—favourite books, the gramophone and records, an old Samurai sword, a train set and a dartboard. The only consolation was that Sono, and not a stranger, would have them.

In the first faint light of dawn a truck drew up in front of the house. It was driven by a Dutch businessman, Mr Hookens, who worked with my father. Sono was already at the gate, waiting to say goodbye.

'I have a present for you,' he said.

He took me by the hand and pressed a smooth hard object into my palm. I grasped it and then held it up against the light. It was a beautiful little sea horse, carved out of pale blue jade.

'It will bring you luck,' said Sono.

'Thank you,' I said. 'I will keep it forever.'

And I slipped the little sea horse into my pocket.

'In you get, lad,' said my father, and I got up on the front seat between him and Mr Hookens.

As the truck started up, I turned to wave to Sono. He was sitting on his garden wall, grinning at me. He called out: 'We will go everywhere, and no one can stop us!'

He was still waving when the truck took us round the bend at the end of the road.

We drove through the still, quiet streets of Batavia, occasionally passing burnt-out trucks and shattered buildings. Then we left the sleeping city far behind and were climbing into the forested hills. It had rained during the night, and when the sun came up over the green hills, it twinkled and glittered on the broad, wet leaves. The light in the forest changed from dark green to greenish gold, broken here and there by the flaming red or orange of a trumpet-shaped blossom. It was impossible to know the names of all those fantastic plants! The road had been cut through dense tropical forest, and on either side, the trees jostled each other, hungry for the sun; but they were chained together by the liana creepers and vines that fed upon the same struggling trees.

Occasionally a Jelarang, a large Javan squirrel, frightened by the passing of the truck, leapt through the trees before disappearing into the depths of the forest. We saw many birds: peacocks, jungle-fowl, and once, standing majestically at the side of the road, a crowned pigeon, its great size and splendid crest making it a striking object even at a distance. Mr Hookens slowed down so that we could look at the bird. It bowed its head so that its crest swept the ground; then it emitted a low hollow boom rather than the call of a turkey.

When we came to a small clearing, we stopped for breakfast. Butterflies, black, green and gold, flitted across the clearing. The silence of the forest was broken only by the drone of airplanes,

Japanese Zeros heading for Batavia on another raid. I thought about Sono, and wondered what he would be doing at home: probably trying out the gramophone!

We ate boiled eggs and drank tea from a thermos, then got back into the truck and resumed our journey.

I must have dozed off soon after, because the next thing I remember is that we were going quite fast down a steep, winding road, and in the distance I could see a calm blue lagoon.

'We've reached the sea again,' I said.

'That's right,' said my father. 'But we're now nearly a hundred miles from Batavia, in another part of the island. You're looking out over the Sunda Straits.'

Then he pointed towards a shimmering white object resting on the waters of the lagoon.

'There's our plane,' he said.

'A seaplane!' I exclaimed. 'I never guessed. Where will it take us?'

'To Bombay, I hope. There aren't many other places left to go to!'

It was a very old seaplane, and no one, not even the captain—the pilot was called the captain—could promise that it would take off. Mr Hookens wasn't coming with us; he said the plane would be back for him the next day. Besides my father and me, there were four other passengers, and all but one were Dutch. The odd man out was a Londoner, a motor mechanic who'd been left behind in Java when his unit was evacuated. (He told us later that he'd fallen asleep at a bar in the Chinese quarter, waking up some hours after his regiment had moved off!) He looked rather scruffy. He'd lost the top button of his shirt, but, instead of leaving his collar open, as we did, he'd kept it together with a large safety pin, which thrust itself out from behind a bright pink tie.

'It's a relief to find you here, guvnor,' he said, shaking my father by the hand. 'Knew you for a Yorkshireman the minute I set eyes on you. It's the *song-fried* that does it, if you know what I mean.' (He meant *sang-froid*, French for a 'cool look.') 'And here I was, with all these flippin' forriners, and me not knowing a word of what they've been yattering about. Do you think this old tub will get us back to Blighty?'

'It does look a bit shaky,' said my father. 'One of the first flying boats, from the looks of it. If it gets us to Bombay, that's far enough.'

'Anywhere out of Java's good enough for me,' said our new companion. 'The name's Muggeridge.'

'Pleased to know you, Mr Muggeridge,' said my father. 'I'm Bond. This is my son.'

Mr Muggeridge rumpled my hair and favoured me with a large wink.

The captain of the seaplane was beckoning to us to join him in a small skiff which was about to take us across a short stretch of water to the seaplane.

'Here we go,' said Mr Muggeridge. 'Say your prayers and keep your fingers crossed.'

The seaplane was a long time getting airborne. It had to make several runs before it finally took off; then, lurching drunkenly, it rose into the clear blue sky.

'For a moment I thought we were going to end up in the briny,' said Mr Muggeridge, untying his seat belt. 'And talkin' of fish, I'd give a week's wages for a plate of fish an' chips and a pint of beer.'

'I'll buy you a beer in Bombay,' said my father.

'Have an egg,' I said, remembering we still had some boiled eggs in one of the travelling bags.

'Thanks, mate,' said Mr Muggeridge, accepting an egg with alacrity. 'A real egg, too! I've been livin' on egg powder these last six months. That's what they give you in the Army. And it ain't hens' eggs they make it from, let me tell you. It's either gulls' or turtles' eggs!'

'No,' said my father with a straight face. 'Snakes' eggs.'

Mr Muggeridge turned a delicate shade of green; but he soon recovered his poise, and for about an hour kept talking about almost everything under the sun, including Churchill, Hitler, Roosevelt, Mahatma Gandhi, and Betty Grable. (The last-named was famous for her beautiful legs.) He would have gone on talking all the way to Bombay had he been given a chance; but suddenly a shudder passed through the old plane, and it began lurching again.

'I think an engine is giving trouble,' said my father.

When I looked through the small glassed-in window, it seemed as though the sea was rushing up to meet us.

The copilot entered the passenger cabin and said something in Dutch. The passengers looked dismayed, and immediately began fastening their seat belts.

'Well, what did the blighter say?' asked Mr Muggeridge.

'I think he's going to have to ditch the plane,' said my father, who knew enough Dutch to get the gist of anything that was said.

'Down in the drink!' exclaimed Mr Muggeridge. 'Gawd 'elp us! And how far are we from Bombay, guv?'

'A few hundred miles,' said my father.

'Can you swim, mate?' asked Mr Muggeridge looking at me.

'Yes,' I said. 'But not all the way to Bombay. How far can you swim?'

'The length of a bathtub,' he said.

'Don't worry,' said my father. 'Just make sure your life-jacket's properly tied.'

We looked to our life-jackets; my father checked mine twice, making sure that it was properly fastened.

The pilot had now cut both engines, and was bringing the plane down in a circling movement. But he couldn't control the speed, and it was tilting heavily to one side. Instead of landing smoothly on its belly, it came down on a wing tip, and this caused the plane to swivel violently around in the choppy sea. There was a terrific jolt when the plane hit the water, and if it hadn't been for the seat belts we'd have been flung from our seats. Even so, Mr Muggeridge struck his head against the seat in front, and he was now holding a bleeding nose and using some shocking language.

As soon as the plane came to a standstill, my father undid my seat belt. There was no time to lose. Water was already filling the cabin, and all the passengers—except one, who was dead in his seat with a broken neck—were scrambling for the exit hatch. The copilot pulled a lever and the door fell away to reveal high waves slapping against the sides of the stricken plane.

Holding me by the hand, my father was leading me towards the exit.

'Quick lad,' he said. 'We won't stay afloat for long.'

'Give us a hand!' shouted Mr Muggeridge, still struggling with his life-jacket. 'First this bloody bleedin' nose, and now something's gone and stuck.'

My father helped him fix the life-jacket, then pushed him out of the door ahead of us.

As we swam away from the seaplane (Mr Muggeridge splashing fiercely alongside us), we were aware of the other passengers in the water. One of them shouted to us in Dutch to follow him.

We swam after him towards the dinghy, which had been released the moment we hit the water. That yellow dinghy, bobbing about on the waves, was as welcome as land.

All who had left the plane managed to climb into the dinghy. We were seven altogether—a tight fit. We had hardly settled down in the well of the dinghy when Mr Muggeridge, still holding his nose, exclaimed: 'There she goes!' And as we looked on helplessly, the seaplane sank swiftly and silently beneath the waves.

The dinghy had shipped a lot of water, and soon everyone was busy bailing it out with mugs (there were a couple in the dinghy), hats, and bare hands. There was a light swell, and every now and then water would roll in again and half fill the dinghy. But within half an hour we had most of the water out, and then it was possible to take turns, two men doing the bailing while the others rested. No one expected me to do this work, but I gave a hand anyway, using my father's sola topi for the purpose.

'Where are we?' asked one of the passengers.

'A long way from anywhere,' said another.

'There must be a few islands in the Indian Ocean.'

'But we may be at sea for days before we come to one of them.'

'Days or even weeks,' said the captain. 'Let us look at our supplies.'

The dinghy appeared to be fairly well provided with emergency rations: biscuits, raisins, chocolates (we'd lost our own), and enough water to last a week. There was also a first aid box, which was put to immediate use, as Mr Muggeridge's nose needed attention. A few others had cuts and bruises. One of the passengers had received a hard knock on the head and appeared to be suffering from a loss of memory. He had no idea how we happened to be drifting about in the middle of the Indian Ocean; he was convinced that we were on a pleasure cruise a few miles off Batavia.

The unfamiliar motion of the dinghy, as it rose and fell in the troughs between the waves, resulted in almost everyone getting seasick. As no one could eat anything, a day's rations were saved.

The sun was very hot, but my father covered my head with a large spotted handkerchief. He'd always had a fancy for bandanna handkerchiefs with yellow spots, and seldom carried fewer than two on his person; so he had one for himself too. The sola topi, well soaked in seawater, was being used by Mr Muggeridge.

It was only when I had recovered to some extent from my seasickness that I remembered the valuable stamp album, and sat up, exclaiming, 'The stamps! Did you bring the stamp album, Dad?'

He shook his head ruefully. 'It must be at the bottom of the sea by now,' he said. 'But don't worry, I kept a few rare stamps in my wallet.' And looking pleased with himself, he tapped the pocket of his bush shirt.

The dinghy drifted all day, with no one having the least idea where it might be taking us.

'Probably going round in circles,' said Mr Muggeridge pessimistically.

There was no compass and no sail, and paddling wouldn't have got us far even if we'd had paddles; we could only resign ourselves to the whims of the current and hope it would take us towards land or at least to within hailing distance of some passing ship.

The sun went down like an overripe tomato dissolving slowly in the sea. The darkness pressed down on us. It was a moonless night, and all we could see was the white foam on the crests of the waves. I lay with my head on my father's shoulder, and looked up at the stars which glittered in the remote heavens.

'Perhaps your friend Sono will look up at the sky tonight and see those same stars,' said my father. 'The world isn't so big after all.'

'All the same, there's a lot of sea around us,' said Mr Muggeridge from out of the darkness.

Remembering Sono, I put my hand in my pocket and was reassured to feel the smooth outline of the jade sea horse.

'I've still got Sono's sea horse,' I said, showing it to my father.

'Keep it carefully,' he said. 'It may bring us luck.'

'Are sea horses lucky?'

'Who knows? But he gave it to you with love, and love is like a prayer. So keep it carefully.'

I didn't sleep much that night. I don't think anyone slept. No one spoke much either, except of course Mr. Muggeridge, who kept muttering something about cold beer and salami.

I didn't feel so sick the next day. By ten o'clock I was quite hungry; but breakfast consisted of two biscuits, a piece of chocolate, and a little drinking water. It was another hot day, and we were soon very thirsty, but everyone agreed that we should ration ourselves strictly.

Two or three still felt ill, but the others, including Mr Muggeridge, had recovered their appetites and normal spirits, and there was some discussion about the prospects of being picked up.

'Are there any distress rockets in the dinghy?' asked my father.

'If we see a ship or a plane, we can fire a rocket and hope to be spotted. Otherwise there's not much chance of our being seen from a distance.'

A thorough search was made in the dinghy, but there were no rockets.

'Someone must have used them last Guy Fawkes Day,' commented Mr Muggeridge.

'They don't celebrate Guy Fawkes Day in Holland,' said my father. 'Guy Fawkes was an Englishman.'

'Ah,' said Mr Muggeridge, not in the least put out. 'I've always said, most great men are Englishmen. And what did this chap Guy Fawkes do?'

'Tried to blow up Parliament,' said my father.

That afternoon we saw our first sharks. They were enormous creatures, and as they glided backward and forward under the boat it seemed they might hit and capsize us. They went away for some time, but returned in the evening.

At night, as I lay half asleep beside my father, I felt a few drops of water strike my face. At first I thought it was the sea spray; but when the sprinkling continued, I realized that it was raining lightly.

'Rain!' I shouted, sitting up. 'It's raining!'

Everyone woke up and did his best to collect water in mugs, hats or other containers. Mr Muggeridge lay back with his mouth open, drinking the rain as it fell.

'This is more like it,' he said. 'You can have all the sun an' sand in the world. Give me a rainy day in England!'

But by early morning the clouds had passed, and the day turned out to be even hotter than the previous one. Soon we were all red and raw from sunburn. By midday even Mr Muggeridge was silent. No one had the energy to talk.

Then my father whispered, 'Can you hear a plane, lad?'

I listened carefully, and above the hiss of the waves I heard what sounded like the distant drone of a plane; but it must have been very far away, because we could not see it. Perhaps it was flying into the sun, and the glare was too much for our sore eyes; or perhaps we'd just imagined the sound.

Then the Dutchman who'd lost his memory thought he saw land, and kept pointing towards the horizon and saying, 'That's Batavia, I told you we were close to shore!' No one else saw anything.

So my father and I weren't the only ones imagining things.

Said my father, 'It only goes to show that a man can see what he wants to see, even if there's nothing to be seen!'

The sharks were still with us. Mr Muggeridge began to resent them. He took off one of his shoes and hurled it at the nearest shark; but the big fish ignored the shoe and swam on after us.

'Now, if your leg had been in that shoe, Mr Muggeridge, the shark might have accepted it,' observed my father.

'Don't throw your shoes away,' said the captain. 'We might land on a deserted coastline and have to walk hundreds of miles!'

A light breeze sprang up that evening, and the dinghy moved more swiftly on the choppy water.

'At last we're moving forward,' said the captain.

'In circles,' said Mr Muggeridge.

But the breeze was refreshing; it cooled our burning limbs, and helped us to get some sleep. In the middle of the night I woke up feeling very hungry.

'Are you all right?' asked my father, who had been awake all the time.

'Just hungry,' I said.

'And what would you like to eat?'

'Oranges!'

He laughed. 'No oranges on board. But I kept a piece of my chocolate for you. And there's a little water, if you're thirsty.'

I kept the chocolate in my mouth for a long time, trying to make it last. Then I sipped a little water.

'Aren't you hungry?' I asked.

'Ravenous! I could eat a whole turkey. When we get to Bombay or Madras or Colombo, or wherever it is we get to, we'll go to the best restaurant in town and eat like—like—'

'Like shipwrecked sailors!' I said.

'Exactly.'

'Do you think we'll ever get to land, Dad?'

'I'm sure we will. You're not afraid, are you?'

'No. Not as long as you're with me.'

Next morning, to everyone's delight, we saw seagulls. This was a sure sign that land couldn't be far away; but a dinghy could take days to drift a distance of thirty or forty miles. The birds wheeled noisily above the dinghy. Their cries were the first familiar sounds we had heard for three days and three nights, apart from the wind and the sea and our own weary voices.

The sharks had disappeared, and that too was an encouraging sign. They didn't like the oil slicks that were appearing in the water.

But presently the gulls left us, and we feared we were drifting away from land.

'Circles,' repeated Mr Muggeridge. 'Circles.'

We had sufficient food and water for another week at sea; but no one even wanted to think about spending another week at sea.

The sun was a ball of fire. Our water ration wasn't sufficient to quench our thirst. By noon, we were without much hope or energy.

My father had his pipe in his mouth. He didn't have any tobacco, but he liked holding the pipe between his teeth. He said it prevented his mouth from getting too dry.

The sharks came back.

Mr Muggeridge removed his other shoe and threw it at them.

'Nothing like a lovely wet English summer,' he mumbled.

I fell asleep in the well of the dinghy, my father's large handkerchief spread over my face. The yellow spots on the cloth seemed to grow into enormous revolving suns.

When I woke up, I found a huge shadow hanging over us. At first I thought it was a cloud. But it was a shifting shadow. My father took the handkerchief from my face and said, 'You can wake up now, lad. We'll be home and dry soon.'

A fishing boat was beside us, and the shadow came from its wide, flapping sail. A number of bronzed, smiling, chattering fishermen—Burmese, as we discovered later—were gazing down at us from the deck of their boat.

A few days later my father and I were in Bombay.

My father sold his rare stamps for over a thousand rupees, and we were able to live in a comfortable hotel. Mr Muggeridge was flown back to England. Later we got a postcard from him, saying the English rain was awful!

'And what about us?' I asked. 'Aren't we going back to England?'

'Not yet,' said my father. 'You'll be going to a boarding school in Simla, until the war's over.'

'But why should I leave you?' I asked.

'Because I've joined the RAF,' he said. 'Don't worry, I'm being posted in Delhi. I'll be able to come up to see you sometimes.'

A week later I was on a small train which went chugging up the steep mountain track to Shimla. Several Indian, Ango-Indian and English children tumbled around in the compartment. I felt quite out of place among them, as though I had grown out of their pranks. But I wasn't unhappy. I knew my father would be coming to see me soon. He'd promised me some books, a pair of roller-skates, and a cricket bat, just as soon as he got his first month's pay.

Meanwhile, I had the jade sea horse which Sono had given me. And I have it with me today.

The Bent-Double Beggar

The person I encounter most often on the road is old Ganpat, the bent-double beggar. Every morning he hobbles up and down the road below my rooms, biding his time, and suddenly manifesting himself in front of unwary passers-by or shoppers. It is difficult to resist Ganpat because, though bent double, he is very dignified. He has a long, white beard and a commanding eye. His voice is powerful and carries well; which is probably why people say he was once an actor.

People say many things about him. One rumour has it that he was once a well-to-do lawyer with a European wife: a paralytic stroke put an end to his career, and his wife finally left him. I have also been told that he is a CID man in disguise—a rumour that might well have been started by Ganpat himself.

I was curious to know the true story of his life, for I was convinced that he was not a beggar by choice; he had little in common with other members of his profession. His English was good, and he could recite passages from Shakespeare; his Hindi was excellent. He never made a direct request for money, but would enter into conversation with you, and remark on the weather or the innate meanness of the human race, until you slipped him a coin.

'Look, Ganpat,' I said one day, 'I've heard a lot of stories about you, and I don't know which is true. How did you become a beggar? How did you get your crooked back?'

'That's a very long story,' he said, flattered by my interest in him. 'I don't know if you will believe it. Besides, it is not to everyone that I would speak freely.'

He had served his purpose in whetting my appetite. I said, 'It will be worth a rupee if you tell me your story.'

He stroked his beard, considering my offer.

'Very well,' he said, squatting down on his haunches, while I pulled myself up on a low wall. 'But it happened more than twenty years ago, and you cannot expect me to remember the details very clearly . . . .'

In those days,' said Ganpat, 'I was a healthy young man, with a wife and baby daughter. I owned a few acres of land, and, though we were not rich, we were not very poor. When I took my produce to the market, five miles away, I harnessed the bullocks and drove down the dusty village road, sometimes returning home late at night.

'Every night I passed a peepul tree, which was said to be haunted. I had never met the ghost, and did not really believe in him, but his name, I was told, was Bippin, and long ago he had been hanged from the peepul tree by a gang of dacoits. Since then this ghost had lived in the tree, and was in the habit of pouncing upon any person who resembled a dacoit and beating him severely. I suppose I must have looked a little guilty after a particularly successful business deal, because one night Bippin decided to pounce on me. He leapt out of the tree and stood in the middle of the road, bringing my bullocks to a halt.

' "You, there," he shouted. "Get off your cart, I am going to thrash you and then string you up from this tree!"

'I was of course considerably alarmed, but decided to put on a bold front. ' "I have no intention of getting off my cart. If you like, you can climb up yourself!"

' "Spoken like a man," said Bippin, and he jumped up beside me. "But tell me one good reason for not stringing you up."

' "I am not a dacoit," I replied.

' "But you look as though you could be one. That is the same thing."

' "I am a poor man, with a wife and child to support."

' "You have no business being poor," said Bippin angrily.

' "Well, make me rich if you can."

' "Do you not believe I can? Do you defy me to make you rich?"

' "Certainly," I said. "I defy you to make me rich."

' "Then drive on," cried Bippin. "I am coming home with you."

'And I drove on to the village with Bippin sitting beside me.

' "I have so arranged it," he said, "that no one will be able to see me. And another thing. I must sleep beside you every night, and no one must know of it. Should you tell anyone about my presence, I will not hesitate to strangle you!"

' "You needn't worry," I said. "I won't tell any one."

' "Good. I look forward to living with you. It was getting lonely in that peepul tree."

'And so Bippin came to live with me, and he slept beside me every night; and we got on very well together. He kept his promise, and money began to pour in from every conceivable source, until I was in a position to buy more land and cattle. Nobody knew of our association, though naturally my friends and relatives wondered where all the money was coming from. At the same time, my wife was rather upset at my unwillingness to sleep beside her at night. I could not very well put her in the same bed with a ghost, and Bippin was most particular about sleeping near me. At first I told my wife that I wasn't well, and that I would sleep on the veranda. Then I told her that there was someone after our cows, and that I would have to keep an eye on them at night. Bippin and I slept in the cow-house.

'My wife would often spy on me at night, suspecting infidelity; but she always found me lying alone amongst the cows. Unable to understand my strange behaviour, she mentioned it to her family; and next day my in-laws arrived on our doorstep, demanding an explanation.

'At the same time my own relatives were insisting that I give them some explanation for my own rapidly increasing fortune. Uncles and aunts and distant cousins descended on me from all parts of the country, wanting to know where the money was coming from, and hoping to have some share of it.

' "Do you all want me to die?" I said, losing my patience with them. "I am under an oath of silence. If I tell you the source of my wealth, I will be signing my own death-warrant."

'But they laughed at me, taking this for a lame excuse; they suspected I was trying to keep my fortune to myself. My wife's relatives suspected that I had found another woman. Finally I became so exasperated with their questions and demands that in a moment of weakness I blurted out the truth.

'They didn't believe the truth (who does?), but it gave them something to think about and talk about, and they left me in peace for a few days.

'But that same night Bippin did not come to sleep beside me. I was left alone with the cows. When he did not come the following night, I was afraid that he would throttle me while I slept. I was almost certain that my good fortune had come to an end, and I went back to sleeping in my own house.

'The next time I was driving back to the village from the market, Bippin leapt out of the peepul tree.

' "False friend," he cried, halting the bullocks. "I gave you everything you wanted, and still you betrayed me!"

' "I'm very sorry," I said. "But as a ghost you wouldn't understand what a man's relatives can be like. You can of course hang me from the peepul tree, if you wish."

' "No, I cannot kill you," he said. "We have been friends for too long. But I must punish you all the same."

'Picking up a stout stick, he struck me three times across the back, until I was bent double.

'After that,' concluded Ganpat, 'I could never straighten myself up again, and for twenty years I have been a crooked man. My wife left me and went back to her family, and I could no longer work in the fields. I left my village and wandered from one city to another, begging for a living. That is how I came here. People in this town seem to be more generous than elsewhere.'

He looked at me with his most appealing smile, waiting for the promised rupee.

'You can't expect me to believe that story,' I said. 'But for your powers of invention you deserve a rupee.'

'No, no,' said Ganpat, backing away and affecting indignation. 'If you don't believe me, keep the rupee!'

Finally he permitted me to force the note into his hand, and then he went hobbling away to the bazaar. I was almost certain he had been telling me a very tall story. But you can never really be sure. Perhaps it was true about Bippin. And it was clever to give him the rupee, just in case he was, after all, a CID man.

Some Teachings of the Bent-Double Beggar:

'A woman can become jealous of anyone, anything,' maintained Ganpat. 'Even of a ghost.'

*

'You must love everyone,' said the bent-double beggar.

'Even my enemies?' I asked.

'It is difficult to love your enemies. Much simpler not to have enemies.'

*

We observed a naked ascetic 'meditating' beneath a peepul tree.

'He is superior to us,' I said. 'He has conquered all desire. We cannot be like that, Ganpat.'

'You think so? Well, let's see. . . .' And approaching the ascetic, he said, 'Babaji, can you teach us to meditate as you do?'

'Yes, I will teach you,' said the other readily. 'It will cost only fifty rupees a lesson.'

'You see?' said Ganpat, turning to me. 'There is indeed some purpose—even desire—in his meditation. I must remember to charge a fee the next time you ask me for advice.'

*

Ganpat the bent-double beggar used to say that if all the troubles in the world could be laid down in one big heap, and everyone was allowed to choose one trouble, we should end up by picking up our old trouble again.

*

He saw in the commonplace what others did not see. A snake. He taught me to see not only the snake, but the path taken by the snake, the beauty of its movements; both the nature of the snake and the nature of the path. He taught me to be that snake, even if it was only for the duration of its passing.

*

'I asked you to my party, but you did not come,' I complained.

'You asked me, that is the important thing. What does it matter if I did not come? You wanted me there, amongst your rich friends. That knowledge gave me all the refreshment I needed.'

In this life all our desires are fulfilled, on the condition that they do not bring the happiness we expected from them.

*

It is no use getting upset about delays in India; they come with unfailing punctuality.

*

His favourite proverb: If you must eat dung, eat elephant's dung.

*

One can forgive ignorance in a man who has had little or no education; but ignorance in a man who has been to college is unforgivable. Yet it is quite common.

*

For democracy to succeed, the first requirement is that the majority of people should be honest.

*

Nietzsche was wrong; it isn't action but pleasure that binds us to existence.

It is difficult to be miserable all the time. Human nature won't permit it. Even when we are burning or burying our dead, we are thinking of what we will eat or drink later in the day.

*

Chance gives, and takes away, and gives again.

*

I travelled a lot once (said Ganpat), but you can go on doing that and not get anywhere. Wherever you go or whatever you do, *most* of your life will have to happen in your mind. And there's no escape from that little room!

Untouchable

The sweeper-boy splashed water over the *khus* matting that hung in the doorway, and for a while the air was cooled.

I sat on the edge of my bed, staring out of the open window, brooding upon the dusty road shimmering in the noon-day heat. A car passed, and the dust rose in billowing clouds.

Across the road lived the people who were supposed to look after me while my father lay in hospital with malaria. I was supposed to stay with them, sleep with them: but except for meals, I kept away. I did not like them and they did not like me.

For a week, longer probably, I was going to live alone in the red-brick bungalow on the outskirts of the town, on the fringe of the jungle. At night the sweeper-boy would keep guard, sleeping in the kitchen. Apart from him, I had no company; only the neighbours' children, and I did not like them and they did not like me.

Their mother said, 'Don't play with the sweeper-boy, he is unclean. Don't touch him. Remember, he is a servant. You must come and play with my boys.'

Well, I did not intend playing with the sweeper-boy; but neither did I intend playing with her children. I was going to sit on my bed all week and wait for my father to come home.

Sweeper-boy . . . all day he pattered up and down between the house and the water-tank, with the bucket clanging against his knees.

Back and forth, with a wide, friendly smile.

I frowned at him.

He was about my age, ten. He had short-cropped hair, very white teeth, and muddy feet, hands, and face. All he wore was an old pair of khaki shorts; the rest of his body was bare, burnt a deep brown.

At every trip to the water tank he bathed, and returned dripping and glistening from head to toe.

I dripped with sweat.

It was supposedly below my station to bathe at the tank, where the gardener, water-carrier, cooks, ayahs, sweepers, and their children all collected. I was the son of a 'sahib' and convention ruled that I did not play with servant children.

But I was just as determined not to play with the other sahibs' children, for I did not like them and they did not like me.

I watched the flies buzzing against the window-pane, the lizards scuttling across the rafters, the wind scattering petals of scorched, long-dead flowers.

The sweeper-boy smiled, and saluted in play. I avoided his eyes, and said, 'Go away.'

He went into the kitchen.

I rose and crossed the room, and lifted my sun helmet off the hat-stand.

A centipede ran down the wall, across the floor.

I screamed and jumped on the bed, shouting for help.

The sweeper-boy darted in. He saw me on the bed, the centipede on the floor; and picking a large book off the shelf, slammed it down on the repulsive insect.

I remained standing on my bed, trembling with fear and revulsion.

He laughed at me, showing his teeth, and I blushed and said, 'Get out!'

I would not, could not, touch or approach the hat or hatstand. I sat on the bed and longed for my father to come home.

A mosquito passed close by me and sang in my ear. Half-heartedly, I clutched at it and missed; and it disappeared behind the dressing-table.

That mosquito, I reasoned, gave the malaria to my father: now it is trying to give it to me!

The next-door lady walked through the compound and smiled thinly from outside the window. I glared back at her.

The sweeper-boy passed with the bucket, and grinned. I turned away.

In bed at night, with the lights on, I tried reading: but even books could not quell my anxiety.

The sweeper-boy moved about the house, bolting doors, fastening windows. He asked me if I had any orders.

I shook my head.

He skipped across to the electric switch, turned off the light, and slipped into his quarters. Outside, inside, all was dark; only one shaft of light squeezed in through a crack in the sweeper-boy's door, and then that too went out.

I began to wish I had stayed with the neighbours. The darkness worried me—silent and close—silent, as if in suspense.

Once a bat flew flat against the window, falling to the ground outside; once an owl hooted. Sometimes a dog barked. And I tautened as a jackal howled hideously in the jungle behind the bungalow. But nothing could break the overall stillness, the night's silence . . . .

Only a dry puff of wind . . . .

It rustled in the trees, and put me in mind of a snake slithering over dry leaves and twigs. I remembered a tale I had been told not long ago, of a sleeping boy who had been bitten by a cobra.

I would not, could not, sleep. I longed for my father . . . .

The shutters rattled, the doors creaked, it was a night for ghosts.

Ghosts!

God, why did I have to think of them?

My God! There, standing by the bathroom door . . . .

My father! My father dead from the malaria, and come to see me!

I threw myself at the switch. The room lit up. I sank down on the bed in complete exhaustion, the sweat soaking my nightclothes.

It was not my father I had seen. It was his dressing-gown hanging on the bathroom door. It had not been taken with him to the hospital.

I turned off the light.

The hush outside seemed deeper, nearer. I remembered the centipede, the bat, thought of the cobra and the sleeping boy; pulled the sheet tight over my head. If I could see nothing, well then, nothing could see me.

A thunderclap shattered the brooding stillness.

A streak of lightning forked across the sky, so close that even through the sheet I saw a tree and the opposite house silhouetted against the flashing canvas of gold.

I dived deeper beneath the bedclothes, gathered the pillow about my ears.

But at the next thunderclap, louder this time, louder than I had ever heard, I leapt from my bed. I could not stand it. I fled, blundering into the sweeper-boy's room.

The boy sat on the bare floor.

'What is happening?' he asked.

The lightning flashed, and his teeth and eyes flashed with it. Then he was a blur in the darkness.

'I am afraid,' I said.

I moved towards him and my hand touched a cold shoulder.

'Stay here,' he said. 'I too am afraid.'

I sat down, my back against the wall; beside the untouchable, the outcaste . . . and the thunder and lightning ceased, and the rain came down, swishing and drumming on the corrugated roof.

'The rainy season has started,' observed the sweeper-boy, turning to me. His smile played with the darkness, and he laughed. And I laughed too, but feebly.

But I was happy and safe. The scent of the wet earth blew in through the skylight and the rain fell harder.

(This was my first short story, written when I was sixteen.)

All Creatures Great and Small

Instead of having brothers and sisters to grow up with in India, I had as my companions an odd assortment of pets, which included a monkey, a tortoise, a python and a Great Indian Hornbill. The person responsible for all this wildlife in the home was my grandfather. As the house was his own, other members of the family could not prevent him from keeping a large variety of pets, though they could certainly voice their objections; and as most of the household consisted of women—my grandmother, visiting aunts and occasional in-laws (my parents were in Burma at the time)—Grandfather and I had to be alert and resourceful in dealing with them. We saw eye to eye on the subject of pets, and whenever Grandmother decided it was time to get rid of a tame white rat or a squirrel, I would conceal them in a hole in the jackfruit tree; but unlike my aunts, she was generally tolerant of Grandfather's hobby, and even took a liking to some of our pets.

Grandfather's house and menagerie were in Dehra and I remember travelling there in a horse-drawn buggy. There were cars in those days—it was just over twenty years ago—but in the foothills a tonga was just as good, almost as fast, and certainly more dependable when it came to getting across the swift little Tons river.

During the rains, when the river flowed strong and deep, it was impossible to get across except on a hand-operated ropeway; but in the dry months, the horse went splashing through, the carriage wheels churning through clear mountain water. If the horse found the going difficult, we removed our shoes, rolled up our skirts or trousers, and waded across.

When Grandfather first went to stay in Dehra, early in the century, the only way of getting there was by the night mail-coach. Mail ponies, he told me, were difficult animals, always attempting to turn around and get into the coach with the passengers. It was only when the coachman used his whip liberally, and reviled the ponies' ancestors as far back as their third and fourth generations, that the beasts could be persuaded to move. And once they started, there was no stopping them. It was a gallop all the way to the first stage, where the ponies were changed to the accompaniment of a bugle blown by the coachman.

At one stage of the journey, drums were beaten; and if it was night, torches were lit to keep away the wild elephants who, resenting the approach of this clumsy caravan, would sometimes trumpet a challenge and throw the ponies into confusion.

Grandfather disliked dressing up and going out, and was only too glad to send everyone shopping or to the pictures—Harold Lloyd and Eddie Cantor were the favourites at Dehra's small cinema—so that he could be left alone to feed his pets and potter about in the garden. There were a lot of animals to be fed, including, for a time, a pair of Great Danes who had such enormous appetites that we were forced to give them away to a more affluent family.

The Great Danes were gentle creatures, and I would sit astride one of them and go for rides round the garden. Inspite of their size, they were very sure-footed and never knocked over people or chairs. A little monkey, like Toto, did much more damage.

Grandfather bought Toto from a tonga-owner for the sum of five rupees. The tonga-man used to keep the little, red monkey tied to a feeding-trough, and Toto looked so out of place there—almost conscious of his own incongruity—that Grandfather immediately decided to add him to our menagerie.

Toto was really a pretty, little monkey. His bright eyes sparkled with mischief beneath deep-set eyebrows, and his teeth, a pearly-white, were often on display in a smile that frightened the life out of elderly Ango-Indian ladies. His hands were not those of a Tallulah Bankhead (Grandfather's only favourite actress), but were shrivelled and dried-up, as though they had been pickled in the sun for many years. But his fingers were quick and restless; and his tail, while adding to his good looks—Grandfather maintained that a tail would add to anyone's good looks—often performed the service of a third hand. He could use it to hang from a branch; and it was capable of scooping up any delicacy that might be out of reach of his hands.

Grandmother, anticipating an outcry from other relatives, always raised objections when Grandfather brought home some new bird or animal; and so for a while we managed to keep Toto's presence a secret by lodging him in a little closet opening into my bedroom wall. But in a few hours he managed to dispose of Grandmother's ornamental wall-paper and the better part of my school blazer. He was transferred to the stables for a day or two, and then Grandfather had to make a trip to neighbouring Saharanpur to collect his railway pension. Anxious to keep Toto out of trouble, he decided to take the monkey along with him.

Unfortunately I could not accompany Grandfather on this trip, but he told me about it afterwards.

A black kit-bag was provided for Toto. When the strings of the bag were tied, there was no means of escape from within, and the canvas was too strong for Toto to bite his way through. His initial efforts to get out only had the effect of making the bag roll about on the floor, or occasionally jump in the air—an exhibition that attracted a curious crowd of onlookers on the Dehra railway platform.

Toto remained in the bag as far as Saharanpur, but while Grandfather was producing his ticket at the railway turnstile, Toto managed to get his hands through the aperture where the bag was tied, loosened the strings, and suddenly thrust his head through the opening.

The poor ticket-collector was visibly alarmed; but with great presence of mind, and much to the annoyance of Grandfather, he said, 'Sir, you have a dog with you. You'll have to pay for it accordingly.'

In vain did Grandfather take Toto out of the bag to prove that a monkey was not a dog or even a quadruped. The ticket-collector, now thoroughly annoyed, insisted on classing Toto as a dog; and three rupees and four annas had to be handed over as his fare. Then

Grandfather, out of sheer spite, took out from his pocket a live tortoise that he happened to have with him, and said, 'What must I pay for this, since you charge for all animals?'

The ticket-collector retreated a pace or two; then advancing again with caution, he subjected the tortoise to a grave and knowledgeable stare.

'No ticket is necessary, sir,' he finally declared. 'There is no charge for insects.'

When we discovered that Toto's favourite pastime was catching mice, we were able to persuade Grandmother to let us keep him. The unsuspecting mice would emerge from their holes at night to pick up any corn left over by our pony; and to get at it they had to run the gauntlet of Toto's section of the stable. He knew this, and would pretend to be asleep, keeping, however, one eye open. A mouse would make a rush—in vain; Toto, as swift as a cat, would have his paws upon him .... Grandmother decided to put his talents to constructive use by tying him up one night in the larder, where a guerrilla-band of mice were playing havoc with our food supplies.

Toto was removed from his comfortable bed of straw in the stable, and chained up in the larder, beneath shelves of jam-pots and other delicacies. The night was a long and miserable one for Toto, who must have wondered what he had done to deserve such treatment. The mice scampered about the place, while he, most uncatlike, lay curled up in a soup tureen, trying to snatch some sleep. At dawn, the mice returned to their holes; Toto awoke, scratched himself, emerged from the soup tureen, and looked about for something to eat. The jam-pots attracted his notice, and it did not take him long to prise open the covers. Grandmother's treasured jams—she had made most of them herself—disappeared in an amazingly short time. I was present when she opened the door to see how many mice Toto had caught. Even the rain-god Indra could not have looked more terrible when planning a thunderstorm; and the imprecations Grandmother hurled at Toto were surprising coming from someone who had been brought up in the genteel Victorian manner.

The monkey was later reinstated in Grandmother's favour. A great treat for him on cold winter evenings was the large bowl of warm water provided by Grandmother for his bath. He would bathe himself, first of all gingerly testing the temperature of the water with his fingers. Leisurely he would step into the bath, first one foot, then the other, as he had seen me doing, until he was completely sitting down in it. Once comfortable, he would take the soap in his hands or feet, and rub himself all over. When he found the water becoming cold, he would get out and run as quickly as he could to the fire, where his coat soon dried. If anyone laughed at him during this performance, he would look extremely hurt, and refuse to go on with his ablutions.

One day Toto nearly succeeded in boiling himself to death.

The large kitchen kettle had been left on the fire to boil for tea; and Toto, finding himself for a few minutes alone with it, decided to take the lid off. On discovering that the water inside was warm, he got into the kettle with the intention of having a bath, and sat down with his head protruding from the opening. This was very pleasant for some time, until the water began to simmer. Toto raised himself a little, but finding it cold outside, sat down again. He continued standing and sitting for some time, not having the courage to face the cold air. Had it not been for the timely arrival of Grandmother, he would have been cooked alive.

If there is a part of the brain especially devoted to mischief, that part must have been largely developed in Toto. He was always tearing things to bits, and whenever one of my aunts came near him, he made every effort to get hold of her dress and tear a hole in it. A variety of aunts frequently came to stay with my grandparents, but during Toto's stay they limited their visits to a day or two, much to Grandfather's relief and Grandmother's annoyance.

Toto, however, took a liking to Grandmother, inspite of the beatings he often received from her. Whenever she allowed him the liberty, he would lie quietly in her lap instead of scrambling all over her as he did on most people.

Toto lived with us over a year, but the following winter, after too much bathing, he caught pneumonia. Grandmother wrapped him in flannel, and Grandfather gave him a diet of chicken soup and Irish stew; but Toto did not recover. He was buried in the garden, under his favourite mango tree.

Perhaps it was just as well that Toto was no longer with us when Grandfather brought home the python, or his demise might have been less conventional. Small monkeys are a favourite delicacy with pythons.

Grandmother was tolerant of most birds and animals, but she drew the line at reptiles. She said they made her blood run cold. Even a handsome, sweet-tempered chameleon had to be given up. Grandfather should have known that there was little chance of his being allowed to keep the python. It was about four feet long, a young one, when Grandfather bought it from a snake-charmer for six rupees, impressing the bazaar crowd by slinging it across his shoulders and walking home with it. Grandmother nearly fainted at the sight of the python curled round Grandfather's throat.

'You'll be strangled!' she cried. 'Get rid of it at once!'

'Nonesense,' said Grandfather. 'He's only a young fellow. He'll soon get used to us.'

'Will he, indeed?' said Grandmother. 'But I have no intention of getting used to him. You know quite well that your cousin Mabel is coming to stay with us tomorrow. She'll leave us the minute she knows there's a snake in the house.'

'Well, perhaps we ought to show it to her as soon as she arrives,' said Grandfather, who did not look forward to fussy Aunt Mabel's visits any more than I did.

'You'll do no such thing,' said Grandmother.

'Well, I can't let it loose in the garden,' said Grandfather with an innocent expression. 'It might find its way into the poultry house, and then where would we be?'

'How exasperating you are!' grumbled Grandmother. 'Lock the creature in the bathroom, go back to the bazaar and find the man you bought it from, and get him to come and take it back.'

In my awestruck presence, Grandfather had to take the python into the bathroom, where he placed it in a steep-sided tin tub. Then he hurried off to the bazaar to look for the snake-charmer, while Grandmother paced anxiously up and down the veranda. When he returned looking crestfallen, we knew he hadn't been able to find the man.

'You had better take it away yourself,' said Grandmother, in a relentless mood. 'Leave it in the jungle across the river-bed.'

'All right, but let me give it a feed first,' said Grandfather; and producing a plucked chicken, he took it into the bathroom, followed, in single file, by me, Grandmother, and a curious cook and gardener.

Grandfather threw open the door and stepped into the bathroom.

I peeped round his legs, while the others remained well behind. We couldn't see the python anywhere.

'He's gone,' announced Grandfather. 'He must have felt hungry.'

'I hope he isn't too hungry,' I said.

'We left the window open,' said Grandfather, looking embarrassed.

A careful search was made of the house, the kitchen, the garden, the stable and the poultry shed; but the python couldn't be found anywhere.

'He'll be well away by now,' said Grandfather reassuringly.

'I certainly hope so,' said Grandmother, who was half way between anxiety and relief.

Aunt Mabel arrived next day for a three-week visit, and for a couple of days Grandfather and I were a little apprehensive in case the python made a sudden reappearance; but on the third day, when he didn't show up, we felt confident that he had gone for good.

And then, towards evening, we were startled by a scream from the garden. Seconds later, Aunt Mabel came flying up the veranda steps, looking as though she had seen a ghost.

'In the guava tree!' she gasped. 'I was reaching for a guava, when I saw it staring at me. The *look* in its eyes! As though it would *devour* me—'

'Calm down, my dear,' urged Grandmother, sprinkling her with eau-de-cologne. 'Calm down and tell us what you saw.'

'A snake!' sobbed Aunt Mabel. 'A great boa-constrictor. It must have been twenty feet long! In the guava tree. Its eyes were terrible. It looked at me in such a *queer* way . . . .'

My grandparents looked significantly at each other, and Grandfather said, 'I'll go out and kill it,' and sheepishly taking hold of an umbrella, sallied out into the garden. But when he reached the guava tree, the python had disappeared.

'Aunt Mabel must have frightened it away,' I said.

'Hush,' said Grandfather. 'We mustn't speak of your aunt in that way.' But his eyes were alive with laughter.

After this incident, the python began to make a series of appearances, often in the most unexpected places. Aunt Mabel had another fit of hysterics when she saw him admiring her from under a cushion. She packed her bags, and Grandmother made us intensify the hunt.

Next morning I saw the python curled up on the dressing-table, gazing at his reflection in the mirror. I went for Grandfather, but by the time we returned the python had moved elsewhere. A little later he was seen in the garden again. Then he was back on the dressing-table, admiring himself in the mirror. Evidently he had become enamoured with his own reflection. Grandfather observed that perhaps the attention he was receiving from everyone had made him a little conceited.

'He's trying to look better for Aunt Mabel,' I said; a remark that I instantly regretted, because Grandmother overheard it, and brought the flat of her broad hand down on my head.

'Well, now we know his weakness,' said Grandfather.

'Are you trying to be funny too?' demanded Grandmother, looking her most threatening.

'I only meant he was becoming very vain,' said Grandfather hastily. 'It should be easier to catch him now.'

He set about preparing a large cage with a mirror at one end. In the cage he left a juicy chicken and various other delicacies, and fitted up the opening with a trap-door. Aunt Mabel had already left by the time we had this trap ready, but we had to go on with the project because we couldn't have the python prowling about the house indefinitely.

For a few days nothing happened, and then, as I was leaving for school one morning, I saw the python curled up in the cage. He had eaten everything left out for him, and was relaxing in front of the mirror with something resembling a smile on his face—if you can imagine a python smiling.... I lowered the trap-door gently, but the python took no notice; he was in raptures over his handsome reflection. Grandfather and the gardener put the cage in the pony-trap, and made a journey to the other side of the river-bed. They left the cage in the jungle, with the trap-door open.

'He made no attempt to get out,' said Grandfather later. 'And I didn't have the heart to take the mirror away. It's the first time I've seen a snake fall in love.'

And the frogs have sung their old song   in the mud .... This was Grandfather's favourite quotation from Virgil, and he used it whenever we visited the rain-water pond behind the house where there were quantities of mud and frogs and the occasional water buffalo. Grandfather had once brought a number of frogs into the house. He had put them in a glass jar, left them on a window-sill, and then forgotten all about them. At about four o'clock in the morning the entire household was awakened by a loud and fearful noise, and Grandmother and several nervous relatives gathered in their night-clothes on the veranda. Their timidity changed to fury when they discovered that the ghastly sounds had come from Grandfather's frogs. Seeing the dawn breaking, the frogs had with one accord begun their morning song.

Grandmother wanted to throw the frogs, bottle and all, out of the window; but Grandfather said that if he gave the bottle a good shaking, the frogs would remain quiet. He was obliged to keep awake, in order to shake the bottle whenever the frogs showed any inclination to break into song. Fortunately for all concerned, the next day a servant took the top off the bottle to see what was inside. The sight of several big frogs so startled him that he ran off without replacing the cover; the frogs jumped out and presumably found their way back to the pond.

It became a habit with me to visit the pond on my own, in order to explore its banks and shallows. Taking off my shoes, I would wade into the muddy water up to my knees, to pluck the water-lilies that floated on the surface.

One day I found the pond already occupied by several buffaloes. Their keeper, a boy a little older than me, was swimming about in the middle. Instead of climbing out on to the bank, he would pull himself up on the back of one of his buffaloes, stretch his naked brown body out on the animal's glistening wet hide, and start singing to himself.

When he saw me staring at him from across the pond, he smiled, showing gleaming white teeth in a dark, sun-burnished face. He invited me to join him in a swim. I told him I couldn't swim, and he offered to teach me. I hesitated, knowing that Grandmother held strict and old-fashioned views about mixing with village children; but, deciding that Grandfather—who sometimes smoked a hookah on the sly—would get me out of any trouble that might occur, I took the bold step of accepting the boy's offer. Once taken, the step did not seem so bold.

He dived off the back of his buffalo, and swam across to me. And

I, having removed my clothes, followed his instructions until I was floundering about among the water-lilies. His name was Ramu, and he promised to give me swimming lessons every afternoon; and so it was during the afternoons—especially summer afternoons when everyone was asleep—that we usually met. Before long I was able to swim across the pond to sit with Ramu astride a contented buffalo, the great beast standing like an island in the middle of a muddy ocean.

Sometimes we would try racing the buffaloes, Ramu and I sitting on different mounts. But they were lazy creatures, and would leave one comfortable spot only to look for another; or, if they were in no mood for games, would roll over on their backs, taking us with them into the mud and green slime of the pond. Emerging in shades of green and khaki, I would slip into the house through the bathroom, bathing under the tap before getting into my clothes.

One afternoon Ramu and I found a small tortoise in the mud, sitting over a hole in which it had laid several eggs. Ramu kept the eggs for his dinner, and I presented the tortoise to Grandfather. He had a weakness for tortoises, and was pleased with this addition to his menagerie, giving it a large tub of water all to itself, with an island of rocks in the middle. The tortoise, however, was always getting out of the tub and wandering about the house. As it seemed able to look after itself quite well, we did not interfere. If one of the dogs bothered it too much, it would draw its head and legs into its shell, and defy all their attempts at rough play.

Ramu came from a family of bonded labourers, and had received no schooling. But he was well-versed in folklore, and knew a great deal about birds and animals.

'Many birds are sacred,' said Ramu, as we watched a bluejay swoop down from a peepul tree and carry off a grasshopper. He told me that both the bluejay and the god Shiva were called *Nilkanth*. Shiva had a blue throat, like the bird, because out of compassion for the human race he had swallowed a deadly poison which was intended to destroy the world. Keeping the poison in his throat, he did not let it go any further.

'Are squirrels sacred?' I asked, seeing one sprint down the trunk of the peepul tree.

'Oh yes, Lord Krishna loved squirrels,' said Ramu. 'He would take them in his arms and stroke them with his long fingers. That is why they have four dark lines down their backs from head to tail.

Krishna was very dark, and the lines are the marks of his fingers.

Both Ramu and Grandfather were of the opinion that we should be more gentle with birds and animals, and should not kill so many of them.

'It is also important that we respect them,' said Grandfather. 'We must acknowledge their rights. Everywhere, birds and animals are finding it more difficult to survive, because we are trying to destroy both them and their forests. They have to keep moving as the trees disappear.'

This was especially true of the forests near Dehra, where the tiger and the pheasant and the spotted deer were beginning to disappear.

Ramu and I spent many long summer afternoons at the pond. I still remember him with affection, though we never saw each other again after I left Dehra. He could not read or write, so we were unable to keep in touch. And neither his people, nor mine, knew of our friendship. The buffaloes and frogs had been our only confidants. They had accepted us as part of their own world, their muddy but comfortable pond. And when I left Dehra, both they and Ramu must have assumed that I would return again like the birds.

Coming Home to Dehra

The faint queasiness I always feel towards the end of a journey probably has its origin in that first homecoming after my father's death.

It was the winter of '44—yes, a long time ago—and the train was running through the thick sal forests near Dehra, bringing me at every click of the rails nearer to the mother I hadn't seen for four years and the stepfather I had seen just once or twice before my parents were divorced.

I was eleven and I was coming home to Dehra.

Three years earlier, after the separation, I had gone to live with my father. We were very happy together. He was serving in the RAF, at New Delhi, and we lived in a large tent somewhere near Humayun's tomb. The area is now a very busy part of urban Delhi but in those days, it was still a wilderness of scrub jungle, where black buck and Nilgai roamed freely. We took long walks together, exploring the ruins of old tombs and forts; went to the pictures (George Formby comedies were special favourites of mine); collected stamps; bought books (my father had taught me to read and write before I started going to school); and made plans for going to England when the war was over.

Six months of bliss, even though it was summer and there weren't any fans, only a thick *khus* reed curtain which had to be splashed with water every hour by a *bhisti* (water-carrier) who did the rounds of similar tents with his goat-skin water bag. I remember the tender refreshing fragrance of the *khus,* and also the smell of damp earth outside, where the water had spilt.

A happy time. But it had to end. My father's periodic bouts of malarial fever resulted in his having to enter hospital for a week. The *bhisti's* small son came to stay with me at night, and during the day I took my meals with an Anglo-Indian family across the road.

I would have been quite happy to continue with this arrangement whenever my father was absent, but someone at Air Headquarters must have advised him to put me in a boarding school.

Reluctantly he came to the decision that this would be the best thing—'until the war is over'—and in the June of '43 he took me to Shimla, where I was incarcerated in a preparatory school for boys.

This is not the story of my life at boarding school. It might easily have been a public school in England; it did in fact pride itself on being the 'Eton of the East'. The traditions—such as ragging and flogging, compulsory games and chapel attendance, prefects larger than life, and Honour Boards for everything from school captaincy to choir membership—had all apparently been borrowed from *Tom Brown's Schooldays*.

My father wrote to me regularly, and his letters were the things I looked forward to more than anything else. I went to him for the winter holidays, and the following summer he came to Shimla during my mid-term break and took me out for the duration of the holidays. We stayed in a hotel called Craig-Dhu, on a spur north of Jacko Hill. It was an idyllic week: long walks; stories about phantom rickshaws; ice-creams in the sun; browsings in bookshops; more plans. 'We will go to England next year.'

School seemed a stupid and heartless place after my father had gone away. He had been transferred to Calcutta and he wasn't keeping well there. Malaria again. And then jaundice. But his last letter sounded quite cheerful. He'd been selling part of his valuable stamp collection so as to have enough money for the fares to England.

One day my class-teacher sent for me.

'I want to talk to you, Bond,' he said. 'Let's go for a walk.'

I knew immediately that something was wrong.

We took the path that went through the deodar forest, past Council Rock where Scout meetings were held. As soon as my unfortunate teacher (no doubt cursing the Headmaster for having given him this unpleasant task) started on the theme of 'God wanting your father in a higher and better place', as though there could be any better place than Jacko Hill in mid-summer, I knew my father was dead, and burst into tears.

They let me stay in the school hospital for a few days until I felt better. The Headmaster visited me there and took away the pile of my father's letters that I'd kept beside me.

'Your father's letters. You might lose them. Why not leave them with me? Then at the end of the year, before you go home, you can come and collect them.'

Unwillingly I gave him the letters. He told me he'd heard from my mother that I would be going home to her at the end of the year. He seemed surprised that I evinced no interest in this prospect.

At the end of the year, the day before school closed, I went to the HM's office and asked for my letters.

'What letters?' he said. His desk was piled with papers and correspondence, and he was irritated by my interruption.

'My father's letters,' I explained. 'I gave them to you to keep for me, Sir—when he died . . . .'

'Letters. Are you sure you gave them to me?'

He grew more irritated. 'You must be mistaken, Bond. Why should I want to keep your father's letters?'

'I don't know, sir. You said I could collect them before going home.'

'Look, I don't remember any letters and I'm very busy just now, so run along. I'm sure you're mistaken, but if I find your letters, I'll send them to you.'

I don't suppose he meant to be unkind, but he was the first man who aroused in me feelings of hate . . . .

As the train drew into Dehra, I looked out of the window to see if there was anyone on the platform waiting to receive me. The station was crowded enough, as most railway stations are in India, with overloaded travellers, shouting coolies, stray dogs, stray station-masters . . . . Pandemonium broke loose as the train came to a halt and people debouched from the carriages. I was thrust on the platform with my tin trunk and small attache case. I sat on the trunk and waited for someone to find me.

Slowly the crowd melted away. I was left with one elderly coolie who was too feeble to carry heavy luggage and had decided that my trunk was just the right size and weight for his head and shoulders. I waited another ten minutes, but no representative of my mother or step-father appeared. I permitted the coolie to lead me out of the station to the tonga stand.

Those were the days when everyone, including high-ranking officials, went about in tongas. Dehra had just one taxi. I was quite happy sitting beside a rather smelly, paan-spitting tonga-driver, while his weary, underfed pony clip-clopped along the quiet tree-lined roads.

Dehra was always a good place for trees. The valley soil is very fertile, the rainfall fairly heavy; almost everything grows there, if given the chance. The roads were lined with neem and mango trees, eucalyptus, Persian lilac, jacaranda, amaltas (laburnum) and many others. In the gardens of the bungalows were mangoes, litchis and guavas; sometimes jackfruit and papaya. I did not notice all these trees at once; I came to know them as time passed.

The tonga first took me to my grandmother's house. I was under the impression that my mother still lived there.

A lovely, comfortable bungalow that spread itself about the grounds in an easygoing, old-fashioned way. There was even smoke coming from the chimneys, reminding me of the smoke from my grandfather's pipe. When I was eight, I had spent several months there with my grandparents. In retrospect it had been an idyllic interlude. But Grandfather was dead. Grandmother lived alone.

White-haired, but still broad in the face and even broader behind, she was astonished to see me getting down from the tonga.

'Didn't anyone meet you at the station?' she asked.

I shook my head. Grandmother said: 'Your mother doesn't live here any more. You can come in and wait, but she may be worried about you, so I'd better take you to her place. Come on, help me up into the tonga. I might have known it would be a white horse. It always makes me nervous sitting in a tonga behind a white horse.'

'Why, Granny?'

'I don't know, I suppose white horses are nervous, too. Anyway, they are always trying to topple me out. Not so fast, driver!' she called out, as the tonga-man cracked his whip and the pony changed from a slow shuffle to a brisk trot.

It took us about twenty-five minutes to reach my stepfather's house which was in the Dalanwala area, not far from the dry bed of the seasonal Rispana river. My grandmother, seeing that I was in need of moral support, got down with me, while the tonga-driver carried my bedding roll and tin trunk on to the veranda. The front door was bolted from inside. We had to knock on it repeatedly and call out, before it was opened by a servant who did not look pleased at being disturbed. When he saw my grandmother he gave her a deferential salaam, then gazed at me with open curiosity.

'Where's the memsahib?' asked grandmother.

'Out,' said the servant.

'I can see that, but where have they gone?'

'They went yesterday to Motichur, for shikar. They will be back this evening.'

Grandmother looked upset, but motioned to the servant to bring in my things. 'Weren't they expecting the boy?' she asked. 'Yes,' he said looking at me again. 'But they said he would be arriving tomorrow.'

'They'd forgotten the date,' said Grandmother in a huff. 'Anyway, you can unpack and have a wash and change your clothes.'

Turning to the servant, she asked, 'Is there any lunch?'

'I will make lunch,' he said. He was staring at me again, and I felt uneasy with his eyes on me. He was tall and swarthy, with oily, jet-black hair and a thick moustache. A heavy scar ran down his left cheek, giving him a rather sinister appearance. He wore a torn shirt and dirty pyjamas. His broad, heavy feet were wet. They left marks on the uncarpeted floor.

A baby was crying in the next room, and presently a woman (who turned out to be the cook's wife) appeared in the doorway, jogging the child in her arms.

'They've left the baby behind, too,' said Grandmother, becoming more and more irate. 'He is your young brother. Only six months old.' I hadn't been told anything about a younger brother. The discovery that I had one came as something of a shock. I wasn't prepared for a baby brother, least of all a baby half-brother. I examined the child without much enthusiasm. He looked healthy enough and he cried with gusto.

'He's a beautiful baby,' said Grandmother. 'Well, I've got work to do. The servants will look after you. You can come and see me in a day or two. You've grown since I last saw you. And you're getting pimples.'

This reference to my appearance did not displease me as Grandmother never indulged in praise. For her to have observed my pimples indicated that she was fond of me.

The tonga-driver was waiting for her. 'I suppose I'll have to use the same tonga,' she said. 'Whenever I need a tonga, they disappear, except for the ones with white ponies . . . . When your mother gets back, tell her I want to see her. Shikar, indeed. An infant to look after, and they've gone shooting.'

Grandmother settled herself in the tonga, nodded in response to the cook's salaam, and took a tight grip of the armrests of her seat. The driver flourished his whip and the pony set off at the same listless, unhurried trot, while my grandmother, feeling quite certain that she was going to be hurtled to her doom by a wild white pony, set her teeth and clung tenaciously to the tonga seat. I was sorry to see her go.

My mother and stepfather returned in the evening from their hunting trip with a pheasant which was duly handed over to the cook, whose name was Mangal Singh. My mother gave me a perfunctory kiss. I think she was pleased to see me, but I was accustomed to a more intimate caress from my father, and the strange reception I had received made me realize the extent of my loss. Boarding school life had been routine. Going home was something that I had always looked forward to. But going home had meant my father, and now he had vanished and I was left quite desolate.

I suppose if one is present when a loved one dies, or sees him dead and laid out and later buried, one is convinced of the finality of the thing and finds it easier to adapt to the changed circumstances. But when you hear of a death, a father's death, and have only the faintest idea of the manner of his dying, it is rather a lot for the imagination to cope with—especially when the imagination is a small boy's. There being no tangible evidence of my father's death, it was, for me, not a death but a vanishing. And although this enabled me to remember him as a living, smiling, breathing person, it meant that I was not wholly reconciled to his death, and subconsciously expected him to turn up (as he often did, when I most needed him) and deliver me from an unpleasant situation.

My stepfather barely noticed me. The first thing he did on coming into the house was to pour himself a whisky and soda. My mother, after inspecting the baby, did likewise. I was left to unpack and settle in my room.

I was fortunate in having my own room. I was as desirous of my own privacy as much as my mother and stepfather were desirous of theirs. My stepfather, a local businessman, was ready to put up with me provided I did not get in the way. And, in a different way, I was ready to put up with him, provided he left me alone. I was even willing that my mother should leave me alone.

There was a big window to my room, and I opened it to the evening breeze, and gazed out on to the garden, a rather unkempt place where marigolds and a sort of wild blue everlasting grew rampant among the litchi trees.

What's Your Dream?

An old man, a beggar man, bent double, with a flowing white beard and piercing grey eyes, stopped on the road on the other side of the garden wall and looked up at me, where I perched on the branch of a litchi tree.

'What's your dream?' he asked.

It was a startling question coming from that raggedy old man on the street; even more startling that it should have been made in English. English-speaking beggars were a rarity in those days.

'What's your dream?' he repeated.

'I don't remember,' I said. 'I don't think I had a dream last night.'

'That's not what I mean. You know it isn't what I mean. I can see you're a dreamer. It's not the litchi season, but you sit in that tree all afternoon, dreaming.'

'I just like sitting here,' I said. I refused to admit that I was a dreamer. Other boys didn't dream, they had catapults.

'A dream, my boy, is what you want most in life. Isn't there something that you want more than anything else?'

'Yes,' I said promptly. 'A room of my own.'

'Ah! A room of your own, a tree of your own, it's the same thing. Not many people can have their own rooms, you know. Not in a land as crowded as ours.'

'Just a small room.'

'And what kind of room do you live in at present?'

'It's a big room, but I have to share it with my brothers and sisters and even my aunt when she visits.'

'I see. What you really want is freedom. Your own tree, your own room, your own small place in the sun.'

'Yes, that's all.'

'That's all? That's everything! When you have all that, you'll have found your dream.'

'Tell me how to find it!'

'There's no magic formula, my friend. If I was a godman, would I be wasting my time here with you? You must work for your dream, and move towards it all the time, and discard all those things that come in the way of finding it, and then, if you don't expect too much too quickly, you'll find your freedom, your room of your own. The difficult time comes afterwards.'

'Afterwards?'

'Yes, because it's so easy to lose it all, to let someone take it away from you. Or you become greedy, or careless, and start taking everything for granted, and—Poof!—suddenly the dream has gone, vanished!'

'How do you know all this?' I asked

'Because I had my dream and lost it.'

'Did you lose everything?'

'Yes, just look at me now, my friend. Do I look like a king or a godman? I had everything I wanted, but then I wanted more and more . . . . You get your room, and then you want a building, and when you have your building you want your own territory, and when you have your own territory you want your own kingdom—and all the time it's getting harder to keep everything. And when you lose it—in the end, all kingdoms are lost—you don't even have your room any more.'

'Did you have a kingdom?'

'Something like that . . . . Follow your own dream, boy, but don't take other people's dreams, don't stand in anyone's way, don't take from another man his room or his faith or his song.' And he turned and shuffled away, intoning the following verse, which I have never heard elsewhere, so it must have been his own.

Live long, my friend, be wise and strong,
But do not take from any man his song.

I remained in the litchi tree, pondering his wisdom and wondering how a man so wise could be so poor. Perhaps he became wise afterwards. Anyway, he was free, and I was free, and I went back to the house and demanded (and got) a room of my own. Freedom, I was beginning to realize, is something you have to insist upon.

The Last Tonga Ride

It was a warm spring day in Dehradun, and the walls of the bungalow were aflame with flowering bougainvillaea. The papayas were ripening. The scent of sweetpeas drifted across the garden. Grandmother sat in an easy chair in a shady corner of the veranda, her knitting needles clicking away, her head nodding now and then. She was knitting a pullover for my father. 'Delhi has cold winters,' she had said; and although the winter was still eight months away, she had set to work on getting our woollens ready.

In the Kathiawar states, touched by the warm waters of the Arabian Sea, it had never been cold but Dehra lies at the foot of the first range of the Himalayas.

Grandmother's hair was white, her eyes were not very strong but her fingers moved quickly with the needles and the needles kept clicking all morning.

When Grandmother wasn't looking, I picked geranium leaves, crushed them between my fingers and pressed them to my nose.

I had been in Dehra with my grandmother for almost a month and I had not seen my father during this time. We had never before been separated for so long. He wrote to me every week, and sent me books and picture postcards; and I would walk to the end of the road to meet the postman as early as possible, to see if there was any mail for us.

We heard the jingle of tonga-bells at the gate, and a familiar horse-buggy came rattling up the drive.

'I'll see who's come,' I said, and ran down the veranda steps and across the garden.

It was Bansi Lal in his tonga. There were many tongas and tonga-drivers in Dehra but Bansi was my favourite driver. He was young and handsome and he always wore a clean white shirt and pyjamas. His pony, too, was bigger and faster than the other tonga ponies.

Bansi didn't have a passenger, so I asked him, 'What have you come for, Bansi?'

'Your grandmother sent for me, *dost.*' He did not call me 'chota sahib' or 'baba', but *'dost'* and this made me feel much more important. Not every small boy could boast of a tonga-driver for his friend!

'Where are you going, Granny?' I asked, after I had run back to the veranda.

'I'm going to the bank.'

'Can I come too?'

'Whatever for? What will you do in the bank?'

'Oh, I won't come inside, I'll sit in the tonga with Bansi.'

'Come along, then.'

We helped Grandmother into the back seat of the tonga, and then I joined Bansi in the driver's seat. He said something to his pony, and the pony set off at a brisk trot, out of the gate and down the road.

'Now, not too fast, Bansi,' said Grandmother, who didn't like anything that went too fast—tonga, motor car, train, or bullock-cart.

'Fast?' said Bansi. 'Have no fear, Memsahib. This pony has never gone fast in its life. Even if a bomb went off behind us, we could go no faster. I have another pony, which I use for racing when customers are in a hurry. This pony is reserved for you, Memsahib.'

There was no other pony, but Grandmother did not know this, and was mollified by the assurance that she was riding in the slowest tonga in Dehra.

A ten-minute ride brought us to the bazaar. Grandmother's bank, the Allahabad Bank, stood near the clock tower. She was gone for about half-an-hour and during this period Bansi and I sauntered about in front of the shops. The pony had been left with some green stuff to munch.

'Do you have any money on you?' asked Bansi.

'Four annas,' I said.

'Just enough for two cups of tea,' said Bansi, putting his arm round my shoulders and guiding me towards a tea stall. The money passed from my palm to his.

'You can have tea, if you like,' I said. 'I'll have a lemonade.'

'So be it, friend. A tea and a lemonade, and be quick about it,' said Bansi to the boy in the teashop and presently the drinks were set before us and Bansi was making a sound rather like his pony when it drank, while I burped my way through some green, gaseous stuff that tasted more like soap than lemonade.

When Grandmother came out of the bank, she looked pensive, and did not talk much during the ride back to the house except to tell me to behave myself when I leant over to pat the pony on its rump. After paying off Bansi, she marched straight indoors.

'When will you come again?' I asked Bansi.

'When my services are required, *dost.* I have to make a living, you know. But I tell you what, since we are friends, the next time I am passing this way after leaving a fare, I will jingle my bells at the gate and if you are free and would like a ride—a fast ride!—you can join me. It won't cost you anything. Just bring some money for a cup of tea.'

'All right—since we are friends,' I said.

'Since we are friends.'

And touching the pony very lightly with the handle of his whip, he sent the tonga rattling up the drive and out of the gate. I could hear Bansi singing as the pony cantered down the road.

Ayah was waiting for me in the bedroom, her hands resting on her broad hips—sure sign of an approaching storm.

'So you went off to the bazaar without telling me,' she said. (It wasn't enough that I had Grandmother's permission!) 'And all the time I've been waiting to give you your bath.'

'It's too late now, isn't it?' I asked hopefully.

'No, it isn't. There's still an hour left for lunch. Off with your clothes!'

While I undressed, Ayah berated me for keeping the company of tonga-drivers like Bansi. I think she was a little jealous.

'He is a rogue, that man. He drinks, gambles, and smokes opium. He has T.B. and other terrible diseases. So don't you be too friendly with him, understand, baba?'

I nodded my head sagely but said nothing. I thought Ayah was exaggerating, as she always did about people, and besides, I had no intention of giving up free tonga rides.

As my father had told me, Dehra was a good place for trees, and Grandmother's house was surrounded by several kinds—peepul, neem, mango, jackfruit, papaya, and an ancient banyan tree. Some of the trees had been planted by my father and grandfather.

'How old is the jackfruit tree?' I asked grandmother.

'Now let me see,' said Grandmother, looking very thoughtful. 'I should remember the jackfruit tree. Oh yes, your grandfather put it down in 1927. It was during the rainy season. I remember, because it was your father's birthday and we celebrated it by planting a tree. 14 July 1927. Long before you were born!'

The banyan tree grew behind the house. Its spreading branches, which hung to the ground and took root again, formed a number of twisting passageways in which I liked to wander. The tree was older than the house, older than my grandparents, as old as Dehra. I could hide myself in its branches behind thick, green leaves and spy on the world below.

It was an enormous tree, about sixty feet high, and the first time I saw it I trembled with excitement because I had never seen such a marvellous tree before. I approached it slowly, even cautiously, as I wasn't sure the tree wanted my friendship. It looked as though it had many secrets. There were sounds and movement in the branches but I couldn't see who or what made the sounds.

The tree made the first move, the first overture of friendship. It allowed a leaf to fall.

The leaf brushed against my face as it floated down, but before it could reach the ground I caught and held it. I studied the leaf, running my fingers over its smooth, glossy texture. Then I put out my hand and touched the rough bark of the tree and this felt good to me. So I removed my shoes and socks as people do when they enter a holy place; and finding first a foothold and then a handhold on that broad trunk, I pulled myself up with the help of the tree's aerial roots.

As I climbed, it seemed as though someone was helping me; invisible hands, the hands of the spirit in the tree, touched me and helped me climb.

But although the tree wanted me, there were others who were disturbed and alarmed by my arrival. A pair of parrots suddenly shot out of a hole in the trunk and, with shrill cries, flew across the garden—flashes of green and red and gold. A squirrel looked out from behind a branch, saw me, and went scurrying away to inform his friends and relatives.

I climbed higher, looked up, and saw a red beak poised above my head. I shrank away, but the hornbill made no attempt to attack me. He was relaxing in his home, which was a great hole in the tree trunk. Only the bird's head and great beak were showing. He looked at me in rather a bored way, drowsily opening and shutting his eyes.

'So many creatures live here,' I said to myself. 'I hope none of them are dangerous!'

At that moment the hornbill lunged at a passing cricket. Bill and tree trunk met with a loud and resonant 'Tonk!'

I was so startled that I nearly fell out of the tree. But it was a difficult tree to fall out of! It was full of places where one could sit or even lie down. So I moved away from the hornbill, crawled along a branch which had sent out supports, and so moved quite a distance from the main body of the tree. I left its cold, dark depths for an area penetrated by shafts of sunlight.

No one could see me. I lay flat on the broad branch hidden by a screen of leaves. People passed by on the road below. A sahib in a sun-helmet. His memsahib twirling a coloured silk sun-umbrella. Obviously she did not want to get too brown and be mistaken for a country-born person. Behind them, a pram wheeled along by a nanny.

Then there were a number of Indians; some in white dhotis some in western clothes, some in loincloths. Some with baskets on their heads. Others with coolies to carry their baskets for them.

A cloud of dust, the blare of a horn, and down the road, like an out-of-condition dragon, came the latest Morris touring car. Then cyclists. Then a man with a basket of papayas balanced on his head. Following him, a man with a performing monkey. This man rattled a little hand-drum, and children followed man and monkey along the road. They stopped in the shade of a mango tree on the other side of the road. The little red monkey wore a frilled dress and a baby's bonnet. It danced for the children, while the man sang and played his drum.

The clip-clop of a tonga pony, and Bansi's tonga came rattling down the road. I called down to him and he reined in with a shout of surprise, and looked up into the branches of the banyan tree.

'What are you doing up there?' he cried.

'Hiding from Grandmother,' I said.

'And when are you coming for that ride?'

'On Tuesday afternoon,' I said.

'Why not today?'

'Ayah won't let me. But she has Tuesdays off.'

Bansi spat red paan-juice across the road. 'Your ayah is jealous,' he said.

'I know,' I said. 'Women are always jealous, aren't they? I suppose it's because she doesn't have a tonga.'

'It's because she doesn't have a tonga-driver,' said Bansi, grinning up at me. 'Never mind. I'll come on Tuesday—that's the day after tomorrow, isn't it?'

I nodded down to him, and then started backing along my branch, because I could hear Ayah calling in the distance. Bansi leant forward and smacked his pony across the rump, and the tonga shot forward.

'What were you doing up there?' asked Ayah a little later.

'I was watching a snake cross the road,' I said. I knew she couldn't resist talking about snakes. There weren't as many in Dehra as there had been in Kathiawar and she was thrilled that I had seen one.

'Was it moving towards you or away from you?' she asked.

'It was going away.'

Ayah's face clouded over. 'That means poverty for the beholder,' she said gloomily.

Later, while scrubbing me down in the bathroom, she began to air all her prejudices, which included drunkards ('they die quickly, anyway'), misers ('they get murdered sooner or later') and tonga-drivers ('they have all the vices').

'You are a very lucky boy,' she said suddenly, peering closely at my tummy.

'Why?' I asked. 'You just said I would be poor because I saw a snake going the wrong way.'

'Well, you won't be poor for long. You have a mole on your tummy, and that's very lucky. And there is one under your armpit, which means you will be famous. Do you have one on the neck? No, thank God! A mole on the neck is the sign of a murderer!'

'Do you have any moles?' I asked.

Ayah nodded seriously, and pulling her sleeve up to her shoulder, showed me a large mole high on her arm.

'What does that mean?' I asked.

'It means a life of great sadness,' said Ayah gloomily.

'Can I touch it ?' I asked.

'Yes, touch it,' she said, and taking my hand, she placed it against the mole.

'It's a nice mole,' I said, wanting to make Ayah happy. 'Can I kiss it?'

'You can kiss it,' said Ayah.

I kissed her on the mole.

'That's nice,' she said.

Tuesday afternoon came at last, and as soon as Grandmother was asleep and Ayah had gone to the bazaar, I was at the gate, looking up and down the road for Bansi and his tonga. He was not long in coming. Before the tonga turned into the road, I could hear his voice, singing to the accompaniment of the carriage bells.

He reached down, took my hand, and hoisted me on to the seat beside him. Then we went off down the road at a steady jog-trot. It was only when we reached the outskirts of the town that Bansi encouraged his pony to greater efforts. He rose in his seat, leaned forward and slapped the pony across the haunches. From a brisk trot we changed to a carefree canter. The tonga swayed from side to side. I clung to Bansi's free arm, while he grinned at me, his mouth red with paan-juice.

'Where shall we go, *dost?*' he asked.

'Nowhere,' I said. 'Anywhere.'

'We'll go to the river,' said Bansi.

The 'river' was really a swift mountain stream that ran through the forests outside Dehra, joining the Ganga about fifteen miles away. It was almost dry during the winter and early summer: in flood during the monsoon.

The road out of Dehra was a gentle decline and soon we were rushing headlong through the tea gardens and eucalyptus forests, the pony's hoofs striking sparks off the metalled road, the carriage wheels groaning and creaking so loudly that I feared one of them would come off and that we would all be thrown into a ditch or into the small canal that ran beside the road. We swept through mango groves, through guava and litchi orchards, past broad-leaved sal and shisham trees. Once in the sal forest, Bansi turned the tonga on to a rough cart-track, and we continued along it for about a furlong, until the road dipped down to the stream bed.

'Let us go straight into the water,' said Bansi. 'You and I and the pony!' And he drove the tonga straight into the middle of the stream, where the water came up to the pony's knees.

'I am not a great one for baths,' said Bansi, 'but the pony needs one, and why should a horse smell sweeter than its owner?' Saying which, he flung off his clothes and jumped into the water.

'Better than bathing under a tap!' he cried, slapping himself on the chest and thighs. 'Come down, *dost*, and join me!'

After some hesitation I joined him, but had some difficulty in keeping on my feet in the fast current. I grabbed at the pony's tail, and hung on to it, while Bansi began sloshing water over the patient animal's back.

After this, Bansi led both me and the pony out of the stream and together we gave the carriage a good washing down. I'd had a free ride and Bansi got the services of a free helper for the long overdue spring-cleaning of his tonga. After we had finished the job, he presented me with a packet of *aam papar*—a sticky toffee made from mango pulp—and for some time I tore at it as a dog tears at a bit of old leather. Then I felt drowsy and lay down on the brown, sun-warmed grass. Crickets and grasshoppers were telephoning each other from tree and bush and a pair of bluejays rolled, dived, and swooped acrobatically overhead.

Bansi had no watch. He looked at the sun and said, 'It is past three. When will that ayah of yours be home? She is more frightening than your grandmother!'

'She comes at four.'

'Then we must hurry back. And don't tell her where we've been, or I'll never be able to come to your house again. Your grandmother's one of my best customers.'

'That means you'd be sorry if she died.'

'I would indeed, my friend.'

Bansi raced the tonga back to town. There was very little motor traffic in those days, and tongas and bullock-carts were far more numerous than they are today.

We were back five minutes before Ayah returned. Before Bansi left, he promised to take me for another ride the following week.

The house in Dehra had to be sold. My father had not left any money; he had never realized that his health would deteriorate so rapidly from the malarial fevers which had grown in frequency; he was still planning for the future when he died. Now that my father had gone, Grandmother saw no point in staying on in India; there was nothing left in the bank and she needed money for our passages to England, so the house had to go. Dr Ghose, who had a thriving medical practice in Dehra, made her a reasonable offer, which she accepted.

Then things happened very quickly. Grandmother sold most of our belongings, because as she said, we wouldn't be able to cope with a lot of luggage. The *kabaris* came in droves, buying up crockery, furniture, carpets and clocks at throwaway prices. Grandmother hated parting with some of her possessions, such as the carved giltwood mirror, her walnut-wood armchair, and her rosewood writing desk, but it was impossible to take them with us. They were carried away in a bullock-cart.

Ayah was very unhappy at first but cheered up when Grandmother got her a job with a tea-planter's family in Assam. It was arranged that she could stay with us until we left Dehra.

We went at the end of September, just as the monsoon clouds broke up, scattered, and were driven away by soft breezes from the Himalayas. There was no time to revisit the island where my father and I had planted our trees. And in the urgency and excitement of the preparations for our departure, I forgot to recover my small treasures from the hole in the banyan tree. It was only when we were in Bansi's tonga, on the way to the station, that I remembered my top, catapult, and Iron Cross. Too late! To go back for them would mean missing the train.

'Hurry!' urged Grandmother nervously. 'We mustn't be late for the train, Bansi.'

Bansi flicked the reins and shouted to his pony, and for once in her life Grandmother submitted to being carried along the road at a brisk trot.

'It's five to nine,' she said, 'and the train leaves at nine.'

'Do not worry, Memsahib. I have been taking you to the station for fifteen years, and you have never missed a train!'

'No,' said Grandmother. 'And I don't suppose you'll ever take me to the station again, Bansi.'

'Times are changing, Memsahib. Do you know that there is now a taxi—a *motor car*—competing with the tongas of Dehra? You are lucky to be leaving. If you stay, you will see me starve to death!'

'We will all starve to death if we don't catch that train,' said Grandmother.

'Do not worry about the train, it never leaves on time, and no one expects it to. If it left at nine o'clock, everyone would miss it.'

Bansi was right. We arrived at the station at five minutes past nine, and rushed on to the platform, only to find that the train had not yet arrived.

The platform was crowded with people waiting to catch the same train or to meet people arriving on it. Ayah was there already, standing guard over a pile of miscellaneous luggage. We sat down on our boxes and became part of the platform life at an Indian railway station.

Moving among piles of bedding and luggage were sweating, cursing coolies; vendors of magazines, sweetmeats, tea and betel-leaf preparations; also stray dogs, stray people and sometimes a stray stationmaster. The cries of the vendors mixed with the general clamour of the station and the shunting of a steam engine in the yards. 'Tea, hot tea!' Sweets, papads, hot stuff, cold drinks, toothpowder, pictures of film stars, bananas, balloons, wooden toys, clay images of the gods. The platform had become a bazaar.

Ayah was giving me all sorts of warnings.

'Remember, baba, don't lean out of the window when the train is moving. There was that American boy who lost his head last year! And don't eat rubbish at every station between here and Bombay. And see that no strangers enter the compartment. Mr Wilkins was murdered *and* robbed last year!'

The station bell clanged, and in the distance there appeared a big, puffing steam engine, painted green and gold and black. A stray dog, with a lifetime's experience of trains, darted away across the railway lines. As the train came alongside the platform, doors opened, window shutters fell, faces appeared in the openings, and even before the train had come to a stop, people were trying to get in or out.

For a few moments there was chaos. The crowd surged backward and forward. No one could get out. No one could get in. A hundred people were leaving the train, two hundred were getting into it. No one wanted to give way.

The problem was solved by a man climbing out of a window.

Others followed his example and the pressure at the doors eased and people started squeezing into their compartments.

Grandmother had taken the precaution of reserving berths in a first-class compartment, and assisted by Bansi and half-a-dozen coolies, we were soon inside with all our luggage. A whistle blasted and we were off ! Bansi had to jump from the running train.

As the engine gathered speed, I ignored Ayah's advice and put my head out of the window to look back at the receding platform. Ayah and Bansi were standing on the platform, waving to me and I kept waving to them until the train rushed into the darkness and the bright lights of Dehra were swallowed up in the night. New lights, dim and flickering came into existence as we passed small villages. The stars too were visible and I saw a shooting star streaking through the heavens.

I remembered something that Ayah had once told me, that stars are the spirits of good men, and I wondered if that shooting star was a sign from my father that he was aware of our departure and would be with us on our journey. And I remembered something else that Ayah had said—that if one wished on a shooting star, one's wish would be granted, provided of course that one thrust all five fingers into the mouth at the same time!

'What on earth are you doing?' asked Grandmother staring at me as I thrust my hand into my mouth.

'Making a wish,' I said.

'Oh,' said Grandmother.

She was preoccupied, and didn't ask me what I was wishing for; nor did I tell her.

Calypso Christmas

My first Christmas in London had been a lonely one. My small bed-sitting-room near Swiss Cottage had been cold and austere, and my landlady had disapproved of any sort of revelry. Moreover, I hadn't the money for the theatre or a good restaurant. That first English Christmas was spent sitting in front of a lukewarm gas-fire, eating beans on toast, and drinking cheap sherry. My one consolation was the row of Christmas cards on the mantelpiece—most of them from friends in India.

But in the following year I was making more money and living in a bigger, brighter, homelier room. The new landlady approved of my bringing friends—even girls—to the house, and had even made me a plum pudding so that I could entertain my guests. My friends in London included a number of Indian and Commonwealth students, and through them I met George, a friendly, sensitive person from Trinidad.

George was not a student. He was over thirty. Like thousands of other West Indians, he had come to England because he had been told that jobs were plentiful, that there was a free health scheme and national insurance, and that he could earn anything from ten to twenty pounds a week—far more than he could make in Trinidad or Jamaica. But, while it was true that jobs were to be had in England, it was also true that sections of local labour resented outsiders filling these posts. There were also those, belonging chiefly to the lower middle-classes, who were prone to various prejudices, and though these people were a minority, they were still capable of making themselves felt and heard.

In any case, London is a lonely place, especially for the stranger. And for the happy-go-lucky West Indian, accustomed to sunshine, colour and music, London must be quite baffling.

As though to match the grey-green fogs of winter, Londoners wore sombre colours, greys and browns. The West Indians couldn't understand this. Surely, they reasoned, during a grey season the colours worn should be vivid reds and greens—colours that would defy the curling fog and uncomfortable rain? But Londoners frowned on these gay splashes of colour: to them it all seemed an expression of some sort of barbarism. And then again Londoners had a horror of any sort of loud noise, and a blaring radio could (quite justifiably) bring in scores of protests from neighbouring houses. The West Indians, on the other hand, liked letting off steam; they liked holding parties in their rooms at which there was much singing and shouting. They had always believed that England was their mother country, and so, despite rain, fog, sleet and snow, they were determined to live as they had lived back home in Trinidad. And it is to their credit, and even to the credit of indigenous Londoners, that this is what they succeeded in doing.

George worked for British Railways. He was a ticket-collector at one of the underground stations; he liked his work, and received about ten pounds a week for collecting tickets. A large, stout man, with huge hands and feet, he always had a gentle, kindly expression on his mobile face. Amongst other accomplishments he could play the piano, and as there was an old, rather dilapidated piano in my room, he would often come over in the evenings to run his fat, heavy fingers over the keys, playing tunes that ranged from hymns to jazz pieces. I thought he would be a nice person to spend Christmas with, so I asked him to come and share the pudding my landlady had made, and a bottle of sherry I had procured.

Little did I realize that an invitation to George would be interpreted as an invitation to all George's friends and relations—in fact, anyone who had known him in Trinidad—but this was the way he looked at it, and at eight o'clock on Christmas Eve, while a chilly wind blew dead leaves down from Hampstead Heath, I saw a veritable army of West Indians marching down Belsize Avenue, with George in the lead.

Bewildered, I opened my door to them; and in streamed George,

George's cousins, George's nephews and George's friends. They were all smiling and shaking hands with me, making complimentary remarks about my room ('Man, that's some piano!' 'Hey, look at that crazy picture!' 'This rocking chair gives me fever!') and took no time at all to feel and make themselves at home. Everyone had brought something along for the party. George had brought several bottles of beer. Eric, a flashy, coffee-coloured youth, had brought cigarettes and more beer. Marian, a buxom woman of thirty-five, who called me 'darling' as soon as we met, and kissed me on the cheeks saying she adored pink cheeks, had brought bacon and eggs. Her daughter Lucy, who was sixteen and in the full bloom of youth, had brought a gramophone, while the little nephews carried the records. Other friends and familiars had also brought beer; and one enterprising fellow produced a bottle of Jamaican rum.

Then everything began to happen at once.

Lucy put a record on the gramophone, and the strains of *Basin Street Blues* filled the room. At the same time George sat down at the piano to hammer out an accompaniment to the record: his huge hands crushed down on the keys as though he were chopping up hunks of meat. Marian had lit the gas-fire and was busy frying bacon and eggs. Eric was opening beer bottles. In the midst of the noise and confusion I heard a knock on the door—a very timid, hesitant sort of knock—and opening it, found my landlady standing on the threshold.

'Oh, Mr Bond, the neighbours—' she began; and glancing into the room was rendered speechless.

'It's only tonight,' I said. 'They'll all go home after an hour. Remember, it's Christmas!'

She nodded mutely and hurried away down the corridor, pursued by something called *Be Bop A-Lula*. I closed the door and drew all the curtains in an effort to stifle the noise; but everyone was stamping about on the floorboards, and I hoped fervently that the downstairs people had gone to the theatre. George had started playing calypso music, and Eric and Lucy were strutting and stomping in the middle of the room, while the two nephews were improvising on their own. Before I knew what was happening, Marian had taken me in her strong arms, and was teaching me to do the calypso. The air, I think, was *Banana Boat Song*.

Instead of the party lasting an hour, it lasted three hours. We ate innumerable fried eggs and finished off all the beer. I took turns dancing with Marian, Lucy, and the nephews. There was a peculiar expression they used when excited. 'Fire!' they shouted. I never knew what was supposed to be on fire, or what the exclamation implied, but I too shouted 'Fire!' and somehow it seemed a very sensible thing to shout.

Perhaps their hearts were on fire, I don't know; but for all their excitability and flashiness and brashness they were lovable and sincere friends, and today, when I look back on my two years in London, that Christmas party is the brightest, most vivid memory of all, and the faces of George and Marian, Lucy and Eric, are the faces I remember best.

At midnight someone turned out the light. I was dancing with Lucy at the time, and in the dark she threw her arms around me and kissed me full on the lips. It was the first time I had been kissed by a girl, and when I think about it, I am glad that it was Lucy who kissed me.

When they left, they went in a bunch, just as they had come. I stood at the gate and watched them saunter down the dark, empty street. The buses and tubes had stopped running at midnight, and George and his friends would have to walk all the way back to their rooms at Highgate and Golders Green.

After they had gone, the street was suddenly empty and silent, and my own footsteps were the only sounds I could hear. The cold came clutching at me, and I turned up my collar. I looked up at the windows of my house, and at the windows of all the other houses in the street. They were all in darkness. It seemed to me that we were the only ones who had really celebrated Christmas.

The Last Time I Saw Delhi

I'd had this old and faded negative with me for a number of years and had never bothered to make a print from it. It was a picture of my maternal grandparents. I remembered my grandmother quite well, because a large part of my childhood had been spent in her house in Dehra after she had been widowed; but although everyone said she was fond of me, I remembered her as a stern, somewhat aloof person, of whom I was a little afraid.

I hadn't kept many family pictures and this negative was yellow and spotted with damp.

Then last week, when I was visiting my mother in hospital in Delhi, while she awaited her operation, we got talking about my grandparents, and I remembered the negative and decided I'd make a print for my mother.

When I got the photograph and saw my grandmother's face for the first time in twenty-five years, I was immediately struck by my resemblance to her. I have, like her, lived a rather spartan life, happy with my one room, just as she was content to live in a room of her own while the rest of the family took over the house! And like her, I have lived tidily. But I did not know the physical resemblance was so close—the fair hair, the heavy build, the wide forehead. She looks more like me than my mother!

In the photograph she is seated on her favourite chair, at the top of the veranda steps, and Grandfather stands behind her in the shadows thrown by a large mango tree which is not in the picture. I can tell it was a mango tree because of the pattern the leaves make on the wall. Grandfather was a slim, trim man, with a drooping moustache that was fashionable in the twenties. By all accounts he had a mischievous sense of humour, although he looks unwell in the picture. He appears to have been quite swarthy. No wonder he was so successful in dressing up 'native' style and passing himself off as a street-vendor. My mother tells me he even took my grandmother in on one occasion, and sold her a basketful of bad oranges. His character was in strong contrast to my grandmother's rather forbidding personality and Victorian sense of propriety; but they made a good match.

But here's the picture, and I am taking it to show my mother who lies in the Lady Hardinge Hospital, awaiting the removal of her left breast.

It is early August and the day is hot and sultry. It rained during the night, but now the sun is out and the sweat oozes through my shirt as I sit in the back of a stuffy little taxi taking me through the suburbs of Greater New Delhi.

On either side of the road are the houses of well-to-do Punjabis, who came to Delhi as refugees in 1947 and now make up more than half the capital's population. Industrious, flashy, go-ahead people. Thirty years ago, fields extended on either side of this road, as far as the eye could see. The Ridge, an outcrop of the Aravallis, was scrub jungle, in which the black buck roamed. Feroz Shah's 14th century hunting lodge stood here in splendid isolation. It is still here, hidden by petrol pumps and lost within the sounds of buses, cars, trucks and scooter-rickshaws. The peacock has fled the forest, the black buck is extinct. Only the jackal remains. When, a thousand years from now, the last human has left this contaminated planet for some other star, the jackal and the crow will remain, to survive for years on all the refuse we leave behind.

It is difficult to find the right entrance to the hospital, because for about a mile along the Panchkuin Road the pavement has been obliterated by tea shops, furniture shops, and piles of accumulated junk. A public hydrant stands near the gate, and dirty water runs across the road.

I find my mother in a small ward. It is a cool, dark room, and a ceiling fan whirrs pleasantly overhead. A nurse, a dark pretty girl from the South, is attending to my mother. She says, 'In a minute,' and proceeds to make an entry on a chart.

My mother gives me a wan smile and beckons me to come nearer. Her cheeks are slightly flushed, due possibly to fever; otherwise she looks her normal self. I find it hard to believe that the operation she will have tomorrow will only give her, at the most, another year's lease on life.

I sit at the foot of her bed. This is my third visit, since I flew back from Jersey, using up all my savings in the process; and I will leave after the operation, not to fly away again, but to return to the hills which have always called me back.

'How do you feel?' I ask.

'All right. They say they will operate in the morning. They've stopped my smoking.'

'Can you drink? Your rum, I mean?'

'No. Not until a few days after the operation.'

She has a fair amount of grey in her hair, natural enough at fifty-four. Otherwise she hasn't changed much; the same small chin and mouth, lively brown eyes. Her father's face, not her mother's.

The nurse has left us. I produce the photograph and hand it to my mother.

'The negative was lying with me all these years. I had it printed yesterday.'

'I can't see without my glasses.'

The glasses are lying on the locker near her bed. I hand them to her. She puts them on and studies the photograph.

'Your grandmother was always very fond of you.'

'It was hard to tell. She wasn't a soft woman.'

'It was her money that got you to Jersey, when you finished school. It wasn't much, just enough for the ticket.'

'I didn't know that.'

'The only person who ever left you anything. I'm afraid I've nothing to leave you, either.'

'You know very well that I've never cared a damn about money. My father taught me to write. That was inheritance enough.'

'And what did I teach you?'

'I'm not sure .... Perhaps you taught me how to enjoy myself now and then.'

She looked pleased at this. 'Yes, I've enjoyed myself between troubles. But your father didn't know how to enjoy himself. That's why we quarrelled so much. And finally separated.'

'He was much older than you.'

'You've always blamed me for leaving him, haven't you?'

'I was very small at the time. You left us suddenly. My father had to look after me, and it wasn't easy for him. He was very sick. Naturally I blamed you.'

'He wouldn't let me take you away.'

'Because you were going to marry someone else.'

I break off; we have been over this before. I am not there as my father's advocate, and the time for recrimination has passed.

And now it is raining outside, and the scent of wet earth comes through the open doors, overpowering the odour of medicines and disinfectants. The dark-eyed nurse comes in again and informs me that the doctor will soon be on his rounds. I can come again in the evening, or early morning before the operation.

'Come in the evening,' says my mother. 'The others will be here then.'

'I haven't come to see the others.'

'They are looking forward to seeing you.' 'They', being my stepfather and half-brothers.

'I'll be seeing them in the morning.'

'As you like . . . .'

And then I am on the road again, standing on the pavement, on the fringe of a chaotic rush of traffic, in which it appears that every vehicle is doing its best to overtake its neighbour. The blare of horns can be heard in the corridors of the hospital, but everyone is conditioned to the noise and pays no attention to it. Rather, the sick and the dying are heartened by the thought that people are still well enough to feel reckless, indifferent to each other's safety! In Delhi there is a feverish desire to be first in line, the first to get anything . . . . This is probably because no one ever gets around to dealing with second-comers.

When I hail a scooter-rickshaw and it stops a short distance away, someone elbows his way past me and gets in first. This epitomizes the philosophy and outlook of the Delhi-*wallah*.

So I stand on the pavement waiting for another scooter, which doesn't come. In Delhi, to be second in the race is to be last.

I walk all the way back to my small hotel, with a foreboding of having seen my mother for the last time.

The Good Old Days

I took Miss Mackenzie an offering of a tin of Malabar sardines, and so lessened the sharpness of her rebuke.

'Another doctor's visit, is it?' she said, looking reproachfully at me over her spectacles. 'I might have been dead all this time. . . .'

Miss Mackenzie, at eighty-five, did not show the least signs of dying. She was the oldest resident of the hill station. She lived in a small cottage halfway up a hill. The cottage, like Longfellow's village of Attri, gave one the impression of having tried to get to the top of the hill and failed halfway up. It was hidden from the road by oaks and maples.

'I've been away,' I explained. 'I had to go to Delhi for a fortnight. I hope you've been all right?'

I wasn't a relative of Miss Mackenzie's, nor a very old friend; but she had the knack of making people feel they were somehow responsible for her.

'I can't complain. The weather's been good, and the padre sent me some eggs.'

She set great store on what was given to her in the way of food. Her pension of forty rupees a month only permitted a diet of dal and rice; but the thoughtfulness of people who knew her and the occasional gift parcel from England lent variety to her diet and frequently gave her a topic of conversation.

'I'm glad you have some eggs,' I said. 'They're four rupees a dozen now.'

'Yes, I know. And there was a time when they were only six annas a dozen.'

'About thirty years ago, I suppose.'

'No, twenty-five. I remember, May Taylor's eggs were always the best. She lived in Fairville—the old house near the Raja's estate.'

'Did she have a poultry farm?'

'Oh no, just her own hens. Very ordinary hens too, not White Leghorns or Rhode Island Reds—but they gave lovely eggs; she knew how to keep her birds healthy . . . . May Taylor was a friend of mine. She didn't supply eggs to just *anybody,* you know.'

'Oh, naturally not. Miss Taylor's dead now, I suppose?'

'Oh yes, quite dead. Her sister saw to that.'

'Oh!' I sensed a story. 'How did that happen?'

'Well, it was a bit of a mystery really. May and Charlotte never did get on with each other and it's a wonder they agreed to live together. Even as children they used to fight. But Charlotte was always the spoilt one—prettier, you see. May, when I knew her was thirty-five, a *good* woman if you know what I mean. She saw to the house and saw to the meals and she went to church like other respectable people and everyone liked her. But Charlotte was moody and bad-tempered. She kept to herself—always had done, since the parents died. And she was a little too fond of the bottle.'

'Neither of them were married?'

'No—I suppose that's why they lived together. Though I'd rather live alone myself than put up with someone disagreeable. Still, they were sisters. Charlotte had been a gay, young thing once, very popular with the soldiers at the convalescent home. She refused several offers of marriage and then when she thought it time to accept someone there were no more offers. She was almost thirty by then. That's when she started drinking—heavily, I mean. Gin and brandy, mostly. It was cheap in those days. Gin, I think, was two rupees a bottle.'

'What fun! I was born a generation too late.'

'And a good thing, too. Or you'd probably have ended up as Charlotte did.'

'Did she get delirium tremens ?'

'She did nothing of the sort. Charlotte had a strong constitution.'

'And so have you, Miss Mackenzie, if you don't mind my saying so.'

'I take a drop when I can afford it—.' She gave me a meaningful look. 'Or when I'm offered . . . .'

'Did you sometimes have a drink with Miss Taylor?'

'I did not! I wouldn't have been seen in her company. All over the place she was, when she was drunk. Lost her powers of discrimination. She even took up with a barber! And then she fell down a *khud* one evening, and broke her ankle!'

'Lucky it wasn't her head.'

'No, it wasn't her own head she broke, more's the pity, but her sister May's—the poor, sweet thing.'

'She broke her sister's head, did she?' I was intrigued. 'Why, did May find out about the barber?'

'Nobody knows what it was, but it may well have been something like that. Anyway, they had a terrible quarrel one night. Charlotte was drunk, and May, as usual, was admonishing her.'

'Fatal,' I said. 'Never admonish a drunk.'

Miss Mackenzie ignored me and carried on.

'She said something about the vengeance of God falling on Charlotte's head. But it was May's head that was rent asunder. Charlotte flew into a sudden rage. She was given to these outbursts, even when sober and brought *something* heavy down on May's skull. Charlotte never said what it was. It couldn't have been a bottle, unless she swept up the broken pieces afterwards. It may have been a heavy—what writers sometimes call a blunt instrument.

'When Charlotte saw what she had done, she went out of her mind. They found her two days later wandering about near some ruins, babbling a lot of nonsense about how she might have been married long ago if May hadn't clung to her.'

'Was she charged with murder?'

'No, it was all hushed up. Charlotte was sent to the asylum at Ranchi. We never heard of her again. May was buried here. If you visit the old cemetery you'll find her grave on the second tier, third from the left.'

'I'll look it up some time. It must have been an awful shock for those of you who knew the sisters.'

'Yes, I was quite upset about it. I was very fond of May. And then, of course, the chickens were sold and I had to buy my eggs elsewhere and they were never so good. Still, those were the days, the good old days—when eggs were six annas a dozen and gin only two rupees a bottle!'

Binya Passes By

While I was walking home one day, along the path through the pines, I heard a girl singing.

It was summer in the hills, and the trees were in new leaf. The walnuts and cherries were just beginning to form between the leaves.

The wind was still and the trees were hushed, and the song came to me clearly; but it was not the words—which I could not follow—or the rise and fall of the melody which held me in thrall, but the voice itself, which was a young and tender voice.

I left the path and scrambled down the slope, slipping on fallen pine needles. But when I came to the bottom of the slope the singing had stopped and no one was there. 'I'm sure I heard someone singing,' I said to myself; but I may have been wrong. In the hills it is always possible to be wrong.

So I walked on home, and presently I heard another song, but this time it was the whistling thrush rendering a broken melody, singing of dark, sweet secrets in the depths of the forest.

I had little to sing about myself, as the electricity bill hadn't been paid, and there was nothing in the bank, and my second novel had just been turned down by another publisher. Still, it was summer, and men and animals were drowsy, and so too were my creditors. The distant mountains loomed purple in the shimmering dust-haze.

I walked through the pines again, but I did not hear the singing. And then for a week I did not leave the cottage, as the novel had to be rewritten, and I worked hard at it, pausing only to eat and sleep and take note of the leaves turning a darker green.

The window opened on to the forest. Trees reached up to the window. Oak, maple, walnut. Higher up the hill, the pines started, and further on, armies of deodars marched over the mountains. And the mountains rose higher, and the trees grew stunted until they finally disappeared and only the black spirit-haunted rocks rose up to meet the everlasting snows. Those peaks cradled the sky. I could not see them from my windows. But on clear mornings they could be seen from the pass on the Tehri road.

There was a stream at the bottom of the hill. One morning, quite early, I went down to the stream, and using the boulders as stepping-stones, moved downstream for about half a mile. Then I lay down to rest on a flat rock, in the shade of a wild cherry tree, and watched the sun shifting through the branches as it rose over the hill called Pari Tibba (Fairy Hill) and slid down the steep slope into the valley. The air was very still and already the birds were silent. The only sound came from the water running over the stony bed of the stream. I had lain there ten, perhaps fifteen minutes, when I began to feel that someone was watching me.

Someone in the trees, in the shadows, still and watchful. Nothing moved; not a stone shifted, not a twig broke; but someone was watching me. I felt terribly exposed; not to danger, but to the scrutiny of unknown eyes. So I left the rock and, finding a path through the trees, began climbing the hill again.

It was warm work. The sun was up, and there was no breeze. I was perspiring profusely by the time I got to the top of the hill. There was no sign of my unseen watcher. Two lean cows grazed on the short grass; the tinkling of their bells was the only sound in the sultry summer air.

That song again! The same song, the same singer. I heard her from my window. And putting aside the book I was reading, I leant out of the window and started down through the trees. But the foliage was too heavy, and the singer too far away for me to be able to make her out. 'Should I go and look for her?' I wondered. Or is it better this way—heard but not seen? For having fallen in love with a song, must it follow that I will fall in love with the singer? No. But surely it is the voice, and not the song that has touched me . . . .' Presently the singing ended, and I turned away from the window.

A girl was gathering bilberries on the hillside. She was fresh-faced, honey-coloured; her lips were stained with purple juice. She smiled at me. 'Are they good to eat?' I asked.

She opened her fist and thrust out her hand, which was full of berries, bruised and crushed. I took one and put it in my mouth. It had a sharp, sour taste. 'It is good,' I said. Finding that I could speak haltingly in her language, she came nearer, said 'Take more then,' and filled my hand with bilberries. Her fingers touched mine. The sensation was almost unique; for it was nine or ten years since my hand had touched a girl's.

'Where do you live?' I asked. She pointed across the valley to where a small village straddled the slopes of a terraced hill.

'It's quite far,' I said. 'Do you always come so far from home?'

'I go further than this,' she said. 'The cows must find fresh grass. And there is wood to gather and grass to cut.' She showed me the sickle held by the cloth tied firmly about her waist. 'Sometimes I go to the top of Pari Tibba, sometimes to the valley beyond. Have you been there?'

'No. But I will go some day.'

'It is always windy on Pari Tibba.'

'Is it true that there are fairies there?'

She laughed. 'That is what people say. But those are people who have never been there. I do not see fairies on Pari Tibba. It is said that there are ghosts in the ruins on the hill. But I do not see any ghosts.'

'I have heard of the ghosts,' I said. 'Two lovers who ran away and took shelter in a ruined cottage. At night there was a storm, and they were killed by lightning. Is it true, this story?'

'It happened many years ago, before I was born. I have heard the story. But there are no ghosts on Pari Tibba.'

'How old are you?' I asked.

'Fifteen, sixteen, I do not know for sure.'

'Doesn't your mother know?'

'She is dead. And my grandmother has forgotten. And my

brother, he is younger than me and he's forgotten his own age. Is it important to remember?'

'No, it is not important. Not here, anyway. Not in the hills. To a mountain, a hundred years are but as a day.'

'Are you very old?' she asked.

'I hope not. Do I look very old?'

'Only a hundred,' she said, and laughed, and the silver bangles on her wrists tinkled as she put her hand up to her laughing face.

'Why do you laugh?' I asked.

'Because you looked as though you believed me. How old are you?'

'Thirty-five, thirty-six, I do not remember.'

'Ah, it is better to forget!'

'That's true,' I said, 'but sometimes one has to fill in forms and things like that, and then one has to state one's age.'

'I have never filled a form. I have never seen one.'

'And I hope you never will. It is a piece of paper covered with useless information. It is all a part of human progress.'

'Progress?'

'Yes. Are you unhappy?'

'No.'

'Do you go hungry?'

'No.'

'Then you don't need progress. Wild bilberries are better.'

She went away without saying goodbye. The cows had strayed and she ran after them, calling them by name: 'Neelu, Neelu!' (Blue) and 'Bhuri!' (Old One). Her bare feet moved swiftly over the rocks and dry grass.

Early May. The cicadas were singing in the forest; or rather, orchestrating, since they make the sound with their legs. The whistling thrushes pursued each other over the tree-tops, in acrobatic love-flights. Sometimes the langurs visited the oak trees, to feed on the leaves. As I moved down the path to the stream, I heard the same singing, and coming suddenly upon the clearing near the water's edge, I saw the girl sitting on a rock, her feet in the rushing water—

the same girl who had given me bilberries. Strangely enough, I had not guessed that she was the singer. Unseen voices conjure up fanciful images. I had imagined a woodland nymph, a graceful, delicate, beautiful, goddess-like creature; not a mischievous-eyed, round-faced, juice-stained, slightly ragged pixie. Her dhoti—a rough, homespun sari—was faded and torn; an impractical garment, I thought, for running about on the hillside, but the village folk put their girls into dhotis before they are twelve. She'd compromised by hitching it up, and by strengthening the waist with a length of cloth bound tightly about her, but she'd have been more at ease in the long, flounced skirt worn in the further hills.

But I was not disillusioned. I had clearly taken a fancy to her cherubic, open countenance; and the sweetness of her voice added to her charms.

I watched her from the banks of the stream, and presently she looked up, grinned, and stuck her tongue out at me.

'That's a nice way to greet me,' I said. 'Have I offended you?'

'You surprised me. Why did you not call out?'

'Because I was listening to your singing. I did not wish to speak until you had finished.'

'It was only a song.'

'But you sang it sweetly.'

She smiled. 'Have you brought anything to eat?'

'No. Are you hungry?'

'At this time I get hungry. When you come to meet me you must always bring something to eat.'

'But I didn't come to meet you. I didn't know you would be here.'

'You do not wish to meet me?'

'I didn't mean that. It is nice to meet you.'

'You will meet me if you keep coming into the forest. So always bring something to eat.'

'I will do so next time. Shall I pick you some berries?'

'You will have to go to the top of the hill again to find the *kingora* bushes.'

'I don't mind. If you are hungry, I will bring some.'

'All right,' she said, and looked down at her feet, which were still in the water.

Like some knight-errant of old, I toiled up the hill again until I found the bilberry bushes; and stuffing my pockets with berries, I returned to the stream. But when I got there I found she'd slipped away. The cowbells tinkled on the far hill.

Glow-worms shone fitfully in the dark. The night was full of sounds—the tonk-tonk of a nightjar, the cry of a barking deer, the shuffling of porcupines, the soft flip-flop of moths beating against the window-panes. On the hill across the valley, lights flickered in the small village—the dim lights of kerosene lamps swinging in the dark.

'What is your name?' I asked, when we met again on the path through the pine forest.

'Binya,' she said. 'What is yours?'

'I've no name.'

'All right, Mr No-name.'

'I mean I haven't made a name for myself. We must make our own names, don't you think?'

'Binya is my name. I do not wish to have any other. Where are you going?'

'Nowhere.'

'No-name goes nowhere! Then you cannot come with me, because I am going home and my grandmother will set the village dogs on you if you follow me.' And laughing, she ran down the path to the stream; she knew I could not catch up with her.

Her face streamed summer rain as she climbed the steep hill, calling the white cow home. She seemed very tiny on the windswept mountainside; a twist of hair lay flat against her forehead, and her torn blue dhoti clung to her firm round thighs. I went to her with an umbrella to give her shelter. She stood with me beneath the umbrella and let me put my arm around her. Then she turned her face up to mine, wonderingly, and I kissed her quickly, softly on the lips. Her lips tasted of raindrops and mint. And then she left me there, so gallant in the blistering rain. She ran home laughing. But it was worth the drenching.

Another day I heard her calling to me—'No-name, Mister
No-name!'—but I couldn't see her, and it was some time before I
found her, halfway up a cherry tree, her feet pressed firmly against
the bark, her dhoti tucked up between her thighs—fair, rounded
thighs, and legs that were strong and vigorous.

'The cherries are not ripe,' I said.

'They are never ripe. But I like them green and sour. Will you
come into the tree?'

'If I can still climb a tree,' I said.

'My grandmother is over sixty, and *she* can climb trees.'

'Well, I wouldn't mind being more adventurous at sixty. There's
not so much to lose then.' I climbed into the tree without much
difficulty, but I did not think the higher branches would take my
weight, so I remained standing in the fork of the tree, my face on a
level with Binya's breasts. I put my hand against her waist, and kissed
her on the soft inside of her arm. She did not say anything. But she
took me by the hand and helped me to climb a little higher, and I put
my arm around her, as much to support myself as to be close to her.

The full moon rides high, shining through the tall oak trees near
the window. The night is full of sounds, crickets, the tonk-tonk of a
nightjar, and floating across the valley from your village, the sound
of drums beating, and people singing. It is a festival day, and there
will be feasting in your home. Are you singing too, tonight? And are
you thinking of me, as you sing, as you laugh, as you dance with your
friends? I am sitting here alone, and so I have no one to think of but
you.

Binya . . . I take your name again and again—as though by taking
it, I can make you hear me, come to me, walking over the moonlit
mountain . . . .

There are spirits abroad tonight. They move silently in the trees;
they hover about the window at which I sit; they take up with the wind
and rush about the house. Spirits of the trees, spirits of the old house.
An old lady died here last year. She'd lived in the house for over thirty
years; something of her personality surely dwells here still. When I
look into the tall, old mirror which was hers, I sometimes catch a

glimpse of her pale face and long, golden hair. She likes me, I think, and the house is kind to me. Would she be jealous of you, Binya?

The music and singing grows louder. I can imagine your face glowing in the firelight. Your eyes shine with laughter. You have all those people near you and I have only the stars, and the nightjar, and the ghost in the mirror.

I woke early, while the dew was still fresh on the grass, and walked down the hill to the stream, and then up to a little knoll where a pine tree grew in solitary splendour, the wind going *hoo-hoo* in its slender branches. This was my favourite place, my place of power, where I came to renew myself from time to time. I lay on the grass, dreaming. The sky in its blueness swung round above me. An eagle soared in the distance. I heard her voice down among the trees; or I thought I heard it. But when I went to look, I could not find her.

I'd always prided myself on my rationality; had taught myself to be wary of emotional states, like 'falling in love', which turned out to be ephemeral and illusory. And although I told myself again and again that the attraction was purely physical, on my part as well as hers, I had to admit to myself that my feelings towards Binya differed from the feelings I'd had for others; and that while sex had often been for me a celebration, it had, like any other feast, resulted in satiety, a need for change, a desire to forget . . . .

Binya represented something else—something wild, dream-like, fairy-like. She moved close to the spirit-haunted rocks, the old trees, the young grass; she had absorbed something from them—a primeval innocence, an unconcern with the passing of time and events, an affinity with the forest and the mountains; this made her special and magical.

And so, when three, four, five days went by, and I did not find her on the hillside, I went through all the pangs of frustrated love: had she forgotten me and gone elsewhere? Had we been seen together, and was she being kept at home? Was she ill? Or had she been spirited away?

I could hardly go and ask for her. I would probably be driven from the village. It straddled the opposite hill, a cluster of slate-roof houses, a pattern of little terraced fields. I could see figures in the fields, but they were too far away, too tiny, for me to be able to recognize anyone. She had gone to her mother's village a hundred miles away, or so, a small boy told me.

And so I brooded; walked disconsolately through the oak forest hardly listening to the birds—the sweet-throated whistling thrush; the shrill barbet; the mellow-voiced doves. Happiness had always made me more responsive to nature. Feeling miserable, my thoughts turned inward. I brooded upon the trickery of time and circumstance; I felt the years were passing by, *had* passed by, like waves on a receding tide, leaving me washed up like a bit of flotsam on a lonely beach. But at the same time, the whistling thrush seemed to mock at me, calling tantalizingly from the shadows of the ravine: 'It isn't time that's passing by, it is you and I, it is you and I . . . .'

Then I forced myself to snap out of my melancholy. I kept away from the hillside and the forest. I did not look towards the village. I buried myself in my work, tried to think objectively, and wrote an article on 'The inscriptions on the iron pillar at Kalsi'; very learned, very dry, very sensible.

But at night I was assailed by thoughts of Binya. I could not sleep. I switched on the light, and there she was, smiling at me from the looking glass, replacing the image of the old lady who had watched over me for so long.

As Time Goes By

P rem's boys are growing tall and healthy, on the verge of manhood. How can I think of death, when faced with the full vigour and confidence of youth? They remind me of Somi and Daljit, who were the same age when I knew them in Dehra during our schooldays. But remembering Somi and Dal reminded me of death again—for Dal had died a young man—and I looked at Prem's boys again, haunted by the thought of suddenly leaving this world, and prayed that I could be with them a little longer.

Somi and Dal . . . . I remember: it was going to rain. I could see the rain moving across the hills, and I could smell it on the breeze. But instead of turning back, I walked on through the leaves and brambles that grew over the disused path, and wandered into the forest. I had heard the sound of rushing water at the bottom of the hill, and there was no question of returning until I had found the water.

I had to slide down some smooth rocks into a small ravine, and there I found the stream running across a bed of shingle. I removed my shoes and socks and started walking up the stream. Water trickled down from the hillside, from amongst ferns and grass and wild flowers; and the hills, rising steeply on either side, kept the ravine in shadow. The rocks were smooth, almost soft, and some of them were grey and some yellow. The pool was fed by a small waterfall, and it was deep beneath the waterfall. I did not stay long, because now the rain was swishing over the sal trees, and I was impatient to tell the others about the pool.

Somi usually chose the adventures we were to have, and I would just grumble and get involved in them; but the pool was my own discovery, and both Somi and Daljeet gave me credit for it.

I think it was the pool that brought us together more than anything else. We made it a secret, private pool, and invited no others. Somi was the best swimmer. He dived off rocks and went gliding about under the water, like a long, golden fish. Dal threshed about with much vigour but little skill. I could dive off a rock too, but I usually landed on my belly.

There were slim silverfish in the waters of the stream. At first we tried catching them with a line, but they usually took the bait and left the hook. Then we brought a bedsheet and stretched it across one end of the stream, but the fish wouldn't come near it. Eventually Somi, without telling us, brought along a stick of dynamite, and Dal and I were startled out of a siesta by a flash across the water and a deafening explosion. Half the hillside tumbled into the pool, and Somi along with it; but we got him out, as well as a good supply of stunned fish which were too small for eating.

The effects of the explosion gave Somi another idea, and that was to enlarge our pool by building a dam across one end. This he accomplished with Dal's and my labour. But one afternoon, when it rained heavily, a torrent of water came rushing down the stream, bursting the dam and flooding the ravine; our clothes were all carried away by the current, and we had to wait for night to fall before creeping home through the darkest alleyways; for we used to bathe quite naked; it would have been unmanly to do otherwise.

Our activities at the pool included wrestling and buffalo-riding. We wrestled on a strip of sand that ran beside the stream, and rode on a couple of buffaloes that sometimes came to drink and wallow in the more muddy parts of the stream. We would sit astride the buffaloes, and kick and yell and urge them forward, but on no occasion did we ever get them to move. At the most, they would roll over on their backs, taking us with them into a pool of slush.

But the buffaloes were always comfortable to watch. Solid, earth-bound creatures, they liked warm days and cool, soft mud. There is nothing so satisfying to watch than buffaloes wallowing in mud, or ruminating over a mouthful of grass, absolutely oblivious to everything else. They watch us with sleepy, indifferent eyes, and tolerate the pecking of crows. Did they think all that time, or did they just enjoy the sensuousness of soft, wet mud, while we perspired under a summer sun . . . ? No, thinking would have been too strenuous for those supine creatures; to get neck-deep in water is their only aim in life.

It didn't matter how muddy we got ourselves, because we had only to dive into the pool to get rid of the muck. In fact, mud-fighting was one of our favourite pastimes. It was like playing snowballs, only we used mud balls.

If it was possible for Somi and Dal to get out of their houses undetected at night, we would come to the pool and bathe by moonlight, and at these times we would bathe silently and seriously, because there was something subduing about the stillness of the jungle at night.

I don't exactly remember how we broke up, but we hardly noticed it at the time. That was because we never really believed we were finally parting, or that we would not be seeing the pool again. After about a year, Somi passed his matriculation and entered the military academy. The last time I saw him, about twenty-five years ago, he was about to be commissioned, and sported a fierce and very military moustache. He remembered the pool in a sentimental, military way, but not as I remembered it.

Shortly after Somi had matriculated, Dal and his family left town, and I did not see him again, until after I returned from England. Then he was in Air Force uniform, tall, slim, very handsome, completely unrecognizable as the chubby little boy who had played with me in the pool. Three weeks after this meeting I heard that he had been killed in an air crash. Sweet Dal . . . I feel you are close to me now . . . I want to remember you exactly as you were when first we met. Here is my diary for 1951*, when I was sixteen and you

---

* This diary formed the nucleus of my first novel, *The Room on the Roof*.

thirteen or fourteen:

7 September: 'Do you like elephants?' Somi asked me.

'Yes, when they are tame.'

'That's all right, then. Daljit!' he called. 'You can come up. Ruskin likes elephants.'

Dal is not exactly an elephant. He is one of us.

He is fat, oh yes he is fat, but it is his good nature that is so like an elephant's. His fatness is not grotesque or awkward; it is a very pleasant plumpness, and nothing could suit him better. If Dal were thin he would be a failure.

His eyes are bright and round, full of mischievousness and a sort of grumpy gaiety.

And what of the pool?

I looked for it, after an interval of more than nearly thirty years, but couldn't find it. I found the ravine, and the bed of shingle, but there was no water. The stream had changed its course, just as we had changed ours.

I turned away in disappointment, and with a dull ache in my heart. It was cruel of the pool to disappear; it was the cruelty of time. But I hadn't gone far when I heard the sound of rushing water, and the shouting of children; and pushing my way through jungle, I found another stream and another pool, and about half-a-dozen children splashing about in the water.

They did not see me, and I kept in the shadow of the trees and watched them play. But I didn't really see them. I was seeing Somi and Daljeet and the lazy old buffaloes, and I stood there for almost an hour, a disembodied spirit, romping again in the shallows of our secret pool. Nothing had really changed. Time is like that.

From Small Beginnings

'And the last puff of the day-wind brought from the unseen villages, the scent of damp wood-smoke, hot cakes, dripping undergrowth, and rotting pine-cones. That is the true smell of the Himalayas, and if once it creeps into the blood of a man, that man will at the last, forgetting all else, return to the hills to die.'

— Rudyard Kipling

On the first clear September day, towards the end of the rains, I visited the pine-knoll, my place of peace and power.

It was months since I'd last been there. Trips to the plains, a crisis in my affairs, involvements with other people and their troubles, and an entire monsoon, had come between me and the grassy, pine-topped slope facing the Hill of Fairies (Pari Tibba to the locals). Now I tramped through late monsoon foliage—tall ferns, bushes festooned with flowering convolvulus—crossed the stream by way of its little bridge of stones—and climbed the steep hill to the pine slope.

When the trees saw me, they made as if to turn in my direction. A puff of wind came across the valley from the distant snows. A long-tailed blue magpie took alarm and flew noisily out of an oak tree. The cicadas were suddenly silent. But the trees remembered me. They bowed gently in the breeze and beckoned me nearer, welcoming me home. Three pines, a straggling oak, and a wild cherry. I went among them, acknowledged their welcome with a touch of my hand against their trunks—the cherry's smooth and polished; the pine's patterned and whorled; the oak's rough, gnarled, full of experience. He'd been there longest, and the wind had bent his upper branches and twisted a few, so that he looked shaggy and undistinguished. But, like the philosopher who is careless about his dress and appearance, the oak has secrets, a hidden wisdom. He has learnt the art of survival!

While the oak and the pines are older than me and have been here many years, the cherry tree is exactly seven years old. I know, because I planted it.

One day I had this cherry seed in my hand, and on an impulse I thrust it into the soft earth, and then went away and forgot all about it. A few months later I found a tiny cherry tree in the long grass. I did not expect it to survive. But the following year it was two feet tall. And then some goats ate its leaves, and a grass cutter's scythe injured the stem, and I was sure it would wither away. But it renewed itself, sprang up even faster; and within three years it was a healthy, growing tree, about five feet tall.

I left the hills for two years—forced by circumstances to make a living in Delhi—but this time I did not forget the cherry tree. I thought about it fairly often, sent telepathic messages of encouragement in its direction. And when, a couple of years ago, I returned in the autumn, my heart did a somersault when I found my tree sprinkled with pale pink blossom. (The Himalayan cherry flowers in November.) And later, when the fruit was ripe, the tree was visited by finches, tits, bulbuls and other small birds, all come to feast on the sour, red cherries.

Last summer I spent a night on the pine-knoll, sleeping on the grass beneath the cherry tree. I lay awake for hours, listening to the chatter of the stream and the occasional tonk-tonk of a nightjar; and watching, through the branches overhead, the stars turning in the sky; and I felt the power of the sky and earth, and the power of a small cherry seed . . . .

And so, when the rains are over, this is where I come, that I might feel the peace and power of this place. It's a big world and momentous events are taking place all the time. But this is where I have seen it happens.

This is where I will write my stories. I can see everything from here—

my cottage across the valley; behind and above me, the town and the bazaar, straddling the ridge; to the left, the high mountains and the twisting road to the source of the great river; below me, the little stream and the path to the village; ahead, the Hill of Fairies, the fields beyond; the wide valley below, and then another range of hills and then the distant plains. I can even see Prem Singh in the garden, putting the mattresses out in the sun.

From here he is just a speck on the far hill, but I know it is Prem by the way he stands. A man may have a hundred disguises, but in the end it is his posture that gives him away. Like my grandfather, who was a master of disguise and successfully roamed the bazaars as fruit-vendor or basket-maker; but we could always recognize him because of his pronounced slouch.

Prem Singh doesn't slouch, but he has this habit of looking up at the sky (regardless of whether it's cloudy or clear), and at the moment he's looking at the sky.

Eight years with Prem. He was just a sixteen-year-old boy when I first saw him, and now he has a wife and child.

I had been in the cottage for just over a year . . . . He stood on the landing outside the kitchen door. A tall boy, dark, with good teeth and brown, deep-set eyes; dressed smartly in white drill—his only change of clothes. Looking for a job. I liked the look of him. But—

'I already have someone working for me,' I said.

'Yes, sir. He is my uncle.'

In the hills, everyone is a brother or uncle.

'You don't want me to dismiss your uncle?'

'No, sir. But he says you can find a job for me.'

'I'll try. I'll make enquiries. Have you just come from your village?'

'Yes. Yesterday I walked ten miles to Pauri. There I got a bus.'

'Sit down. Your uncle will make some tea.'

He sat down on the steps, removed his white keds, wriggled his toes. His feet were both long and broad; large feet, but not ugly. He was unusually clean for a hill boy. And taller than most.

'Do you smoke?' I asked.

'No, sir.'

'It is true,' said his uncle, 'he does not smoke. All my nephews smoke, but this one, he is a little peculiar, he does not smoke—neither *beedi* nor hookah.'

'Do you drink?'

'It makes me vomit.'

'Do you take bhang?'

'No, sahib.'

'You have no vices. It's unnatural.'

'He is unnatural, sahib,' said his uncle.

'Does he chase girls?'

'They chase him, sahib.'

'So he left the village and came looking for a job.' I looked at him. He grinned, then looked away, began rubbing his feet.

'Your name is?'

'Prem Singh.'

'All right, Prem, I will try to do something for you.'

I did not see him for a couple of weeks. I forgot about finding him a job. But when I met him again, on the road to the bazaar, he told me that he had got a temporary job in the Survey, looking after the surveyor's tents.

'Next week we will be going to Rajasthan,' he said.

'It will be very hot. Have you been in the desert before?'

'No, sir.'

'It is not like the hills. And it is far from home.'

'I know. But I have no choice in the matter. I have to collect some money in order to get married.'

In his region there was a bride price, usually of two thousand rupees.

'Do you have to get married so soon?'

'I have only one brother and he is still very young. My mother is not well. She needs a daughter-in-law to help her in the fields and with the cows and in the house. We are a small family, so the work is greater.'

Every family has its few terraced fields, narrow and stony, usually perched on a hillside above a stream or river. They grow rice, barley, maize, potatoes—just enough to live on. Even if they produced sufficient for marketing, the absence of roads makes it difficult to get the produce to the market towns. There is no money to be earned in the villages, and money is needed for clothes, soap, medicines, and recovering the family jewellery from the money-lenders. So the young men leave their villages to find work, and to find work they must go to the plains. The lucky ones get into the Army. Others enter domestic service or take jobs in garages, hotels, wayside teashops, schools . . . .

In Mussoorie the main attraction is the large number of schools, which employ cooks and bearers. But the schools were full when Prem arrived. He'd been to the recruiting centre at Roorkee, hoping to get into the Army; but they found a deformity in his right foot, the result of a bone broken when a landslip carried him away one dark monsoon night; he was lucky, he said, that it was only his foot and not his head that had been broken.

He came to the house to inform his uncle about the job and to say goodbye. I thought: another nice person I probably won't see again; another ship passing in the night, the friendly twinkle of its lights soon vanishing in the darkness. I said 'Come again', held his smile with mine so that I could remember him better, and returned to my study and my typewriter. The typewriter is the repository of a writer's loneliness. It stares unsympathetically back at him every day, doing its best to be discouraging. Maybe I'll go back to the old-fashioned quill pen and a marble ink-stand; then I can feel like a real writer, Balzac or Dickens, scratching away into the endless reaches of the night . . . . Of course, the days and nights are seemingly shorter than they need to be! They must be, otherwise why do we hurry so much and achieve so little, by the standards of the past . . . .

Prem goes, disappears into the vast faceless cities of the plains, and a year slips by, or rather I do, and then here he is again, thinner and darker and still smiling and still looking for a job. I should have known that hill men don't disappear for ever. The spirit-haunted rocks don't let their people wander too far, lest they lose them forever.

I was able to get him a job in the school. The Headmaster's wife needed a cook. I wasn't sure if Prem could cook very well but I sent him along and they said they'd give him a trial. Three days later the Headmaster's wife met me on the road and started gushing all over me. She was the type who gushes.

'We're so grateful to you! Thank you for sending me that lovely boy. He's so polite. And he cooks very well. A little too hot for my husband, but otherwise delicious—just delicious! He's a real treasure—a lovely boy.' And she gave me an arch look—the famous look which she used to captivate all the good-looking young prefects who became prefects, it was said, only if she approved of them.

I wasn't sure if she didn't want something more than a cook, and I only hoped that Prem would give every satisfaction.

He looked cheerful enough when he came to see me on his off-day.

'How are you getting on?' I asked.

'Lovely,' he said, using his mistress's favourite expression.

'What do you mean—lovely? Do they like your work?'

'The memsahib likes it. She strokes me on the cheek whenever she enters the kitchen. The sahib says nothing. He takes medicine after every meal.'

'Did he always take medicine—or only now that you're doing the cooking?'

'I am not sure. I think he has always been sick.'

He was sleeping in the Headmaster's veranda and getting sixty rupees a month. A cook in Delhi got a hundred and sixty. And a cook in Paris or New York got ten times as much. I did not say as much to Prem. He might ask me to get him a job in New York. And that would be the last I saw of him! He, as a cook, might well get a job making curries off Broadway; I, as a writer, wouldn't get to first base. And only my Uncle Ken knew the secret of how to make a living without actually doing any work. But then, of course, he had four sisters. And each of them was married to a fairly prosperous husband. So Uncle Ken divided up his year among them. Three months with Aunt Ruby in Nainital. Three months with Aunt Susie in Kashmir. Three months with my mother (not quite so affluent) in Jamnagar. And three months in the Vet Hospital in Bareilly, where Aunt Mabel ran the hospital for her veterinary husband. In this way he never overstayed his welcome. A sister can look after a brother for just three months at a time and no more. Uncle K had it worked out to perfection.

But I had no sisters, and I couldn't live forever on the royalties of a single novel. So I had to write others. So I came to the hills.

The hill men go to the plains to make a living. I had to come to the hills to try and make mine.

'Prem,' I said. 'Why don't you work for me.'

'And what about my uncle?'

'He seems ready to desert me any day. His grandfather is ill, he says, and he wants to go home.'

'His grandfather died last year.'

'That's what I mean—he's getting restless. And I don't mind if he goes. These days he seems to be suffering from a form of sleeping sickness. I have to get up first and make his tea . . . .'

Sitting here under the cherry tree, whose leaves are just beginning to turn yellow, I rest my chin on my knees and gaze across the valley to where Prem moves about in the garden. Looking back over the seven years he has been with me, I recall some of the nicest things about him. They come to me in no particular order—just pieces of cinema—coloured slides slipping across the screen of memory . . . .

Prem rocking his infant son to sleep—crooning to him, passing his large hand gently over the child's curly head—Prem following me down to the police-station when I was arrested*, and waiting outside until I reappeared—his smile, when I found him in Delhi—his large, irrepressible laughter, most in evidence when he was seeing an old Laurel and Hardy movie.

Of course there were times when he could be infuriating, stubborn, deliberately pig-headed, sending me little notes of resignation—but I never found it difficult to overlook these little acts of self-indulgence. He had brought much love and laughter into my life, and what more could a lonely man ask for?

It was his stubborn streak that limited the length of his stay in the Headmaster's household. Mr Good was tolerant enough. But Mrs Good was one of those women who, when they are pleased with you, go out of their way to help, pamper and flatter; and who, when they are displeased, become vindictive, going out of their way to harm or destroy. Mrs Good sought power—over her husband, her dog, her favourite pupils, her servant . . . . She had absolute power over the husband and the dog; partial power over her slightly bewildered pupils; and none at all over Prem, who missed the subtleties of her designs upon his soul. He did not respond to her mothering; or to the way in which she tweaked him on the cheeks, brushed against him in the kitchen, or made admiring remarks about his looks and

---

* On a warrant from Bombay, charging me with writing an allegedly obcene short story!

physique. Memsahibs, he knew, were not for him. So he kept a stony face and went diligently about his duties. And she felt slighted, put in her place. Her liking turned to dislike. Instead of admiring remarks, she began making disparaging remarks about his looks, his clothes, his manners. She found fault with his cooking. No longer was it 'lovely'. She even accused him of taking away the dog's meat and giving it to a poor family living on the hillside: no more heinous crime could be imagined! Mr Good threatened him with dismissal. So Prem became stubborn. The following day he withheld the dog's food altogether; threw it down the *khud* where it was seized upon by innumerable strays; and went off to the pictures.

It was the end of his job. 'I'll have to go home now,' he told me. 'I won't get another job in this area. The Mem will see to that.'

'Stay a few days,' I said.

'I have only enough money with which to get home.'

'Keep it for going home. You can stay with me for a few days, while you look around. Your uncle won't mind sharing his food with you.'

His uncle did mind. He did not like the idea of working for his nephew as well; it seemed to him no part of his duties. And he was apprehensive lest Prem might get his job.

So Prem stayed no longer than a week.

Here on the knoll the grass is just beginning to turn October yellow. The first clouds approaching winter cover the sky. The trees are very still. The birds are silent. Only a cricket keeps singing on the oak tree. Perhaps there will be a storm before evening. A storm like that in which Prem arrived at the cottage with his wife and child—but that's jumping too far ahead . . . .

After he had returned to his village, it was several months before I saw him again. His uncle told me he had taken a job in Delhi. There was an address. It did not seem complete, but I resolved that when I was next in Delhi, I would try to see him.

The opportunity came in May, as the hot winds of summer blew across the plains. It was the time of year when people who can afford it, try to get away to the hills. I dislike New Delhi at the best of times, and I hate it in summer. People compete with each other in being bad-tempered and mean. But I had to go down—I don't remember why, but it must have seemed very necessary at the time—and I took the opportunity to try and see Prem.

Nothing went right for me. Of course the address was all wrong, and I wandered about in a remote, dusty, treeless colony called Vasant Vihar (Spring Garden) for over two hours, asking all the domestic servants I came across if they could put me in touch with Prem Singh of Village Koli, Pauri Garhwal. There were innumerable Prem Singhs, but apparently none who belonged to Village Koli. I returned to my hotel and took two days to recover from heatstroke before returning to Mussoorie, thanking God for mountains!

And then the uncle gave me notice. He'd found a better-paid job in Dehradun and was anxious to be off. I didn't try to stop him.

For the next six months I lived in the cottage without any help. I did not find this difficult. I was used to living alone. It wasn't service that I needed but companionship. In the cottage it was very quiet. The ghosts of long dead residents were sympathetic but unobtrusive. The song of the whistling thrush was beautiful, but I knew he was not singing for me. Up the valley came the sound of a flute, but I never saw the flute player. My affinity was with the little red fox who roamed the hillside below the cottage. I met him one night and wrote these lines:

> As I walked home last night
> I saw a lone fox dancing
> In the cold moonlight.
> I stood and watched—then
> Took the low road, knowing
> The night was his by right.
> Sometimes, when words ring true,
> I'm like a lone fox dancing
> In the morning dew.

During the rains, watching the dripping trees and the mist climbing the valley, I wrote a great deal of poetry. Loneliness is of value to poets. But poetry didn't bring me much money, and funds were low.

And then, just as I was wondering if I would have to give up my freedom and take a job again, a publisher bought the paperback rights of one of my children's stories, and I was free to live and write as I pleased—for another three months!

That was in November. To celebrate, I took a long walk through the Landour Bazaar and up the Tehri road. It was a good day for walking; and it was dark by the time I returned to the outskirts of the town. Someone stood waiting for me on the road above the cottage. I hurried past him.

> *If I am not for myself,*
> *Who will be for me?*
> *And if I am not for others,*
> *What am I?*
> *And if not now, when?*

I startled myself with the memory of these words of Hillel, the ancient Hebrew sage. I walked back to the shadows where the youth stood, and saw that it was Prem.

'Prem!' I said. 'Why are you sitting out here, in the cold? Why did you not go to the house?'

'I went, sir, but there was a lock on the door. I thought you had gone away.'

'And you were going to remain here, on the road?'

'Only for tonight. I would have gone down to Dehra in the morning.'

'Come, let's go home. I have been waiting for you. I looked for you in Delhi, but could not find the place where you were working.'

'I have left them now.'

'And your uncle has left me. So will you work for me now?'

'For as long as you wish,'

'For as long as the gods wish.'

We did not go straight home, but returned to the bazaar and took our meal in the Sindhi Sweet Shop; hot puris and strong sweet tea.

We walked home together in the bright moonlight. I felt sorry for the little fox, dancing alone.

That was twenty years ago, and Prem and his wife and three children are still with me. But we live in a different house now, on another hill.

Death of the Trees

The peace and quiet of the Maplewood hillside disappeared forever one winter. The powers-that-be decided to build another new road into the mountains, and the PWD saw fit to take it right past the cottage, about six feet from the large window which had overlooked the forest.

In my journal I wrote: already they have felled most of the trees. The walnut was one of the first to go. A tree I had lived with for over ten years, watching it grow just as I had watched Prem's little son, Rakesh, grow up.... Looking forward to its new leaf-buds, the broad, green leaves of summer, turning to spears of gold in September when the walnuts were ripe and ready to fall. I knew this tree better than the others. It was just below the window, where a buttress for the road is going up.

Another tree I'll miss is the young deodar, the only one growing in this stretch of the woods. Some years back it was stunted from lack of sunlight. The oaks covered it with their shaggy branches. So I cut away some of the overhanging branches and after that the deodar grew much faster. It was just coming into its own this year; now cut down in its prime like my young brother on the road to Delhi last month: both victims of the roads. The tree killed by the PWD; my brother by a truck.

Twenty oaks have been felled. Just in this small stretch near the cottage. By the time this bypass reaches Jabarkhet, about six miles from here, over a thousand oaks will have been slaughtered, besides many other fine trees—maples, deodars and pines—most of them unnecessarily, as they grew some fifty to sixty yards from the roadside.

The trouble is, hardly anyone (with the exception of the contractor who buys the felled trees) really believes that trees and shrubs are necessary. They get in the way so much, don't they? According to my milkman, the only useful tree is one which can be picked clean of its leaves for fodder! And a young man remarked to me: 'You should come to Pauri. The view is terrific, there are no trees in the way!'

Well, he can stay here now, and enjoy the view of the ravaged hillside. But as the oaks have gone, the milkman will have to look further afield for his fodder.

Rakesh calls the maples the butterfly trees because, when the winged seeds fall, they flutter like butterflies in the breeze. No maples now. No bright red leaves to flame against the sky. No birds!

That is to say, no birds near the house. No longer will it be possible for me to open the window and watch the scarlet minivets flitting through the dark green foliage of the oaks; the long-tailed magpies gliding through the trees; the barbet calling insistently from his perch on top of the deodar. Forest birds, all of them, they will now be in search of some other stretch of surviving forest. The only visitors will be the crows, who have learnt to live with, and off, humans, and seem to multiply along with roads, houses and people. And even when all the people have gone, the crows will still be around.

Other things to look forward to: trucks thundering past in the night; perhaps a tea and pakora shop around the corner; the grinding of gears, the music of motor horns. Will the whistling thrush be heard above them? The explosions that continually shatter the silence of the mountains, as thousand-year-old rocks are dynamited, have frightened away all but the most intrepid of birds and animals. Even the bold langurs haven't shown their faces for over a fortnight.

Somehow, I don't think we shall wait for the tea shop to arrive. There must be some other quiet corner, possibly on the next mountain, where new roads have yet to come into being. No doubt this is a negative attitude, and if I had any sense I'd open my own tea shop. To retreat is to be a loser. But the trees are losers too; and when they fall, they do so with a certain dignity.

Never mind. Men come and go; the mountains remain.

A Flight of Pigeons

Prologue

The revolt broke out at Meerut on the 10th of May, at the beginning of a very hot and oppressive summer. The sepoys shot down their English officers; there was rioting and looting in the city; the jail was broken open, and armed convicts descended on English families living in the city and cantonment, setting fire to houses and killing the inmates. Several mutinous regiments marched to Delhi, their principal rallying-point, where the peaceable, poetry-loving Emperor Bahadur Shah, suddenly found himself the figurehead of the revolt.

The British Army, which had been cooling off in Shimla, began its long march to Delhi. But meanwhile, the conflict had spread to other cities. And on the 30th of May there was much excitement in the magistrate's office at Shahjahanpur, some 250 miles east of Delhi.

A bungalow in the cantonment, owned by the Redmans, an Anglo-Indian family, had been set on fire during the night. The Redmans had been able to escape, but most of their property was looted or destroyed. A familiar figure had been seen flitting around the grounds that night; and Javed Khan, a Rohilla Pathan, well-known to everyone in the city, was arrested on suspicion of arson and brought before the magistrate.

Javed Khan was a person of some importance in the bazaars of Shahjahanpur. He had a reputation for being willing to undertake any exploit of a dangerous nature, provided the rewards were high. He had been brought in by the authorities for a number of offences. But Javed knew the English law, and challenged the court to produce witnesses. None came forward to identify him as the man who had been seen running from the blazing bungalow. The case was adjourned until further evidence could be collected. When Javed left the courtroom, it was difficult to tell whether he was being escorted by the police or whether he was escorting them. Before leaving the room, he bowed contemptuously to Mr Ricketts, the magistrate, and said: '*My* witnesses will be produced tomorrow, whether you will have them or not.'

The burning of the Redmans' bungalow failed to alert the small English community in Shahjahanpur to a sense of danger. Meerut was far away, and the *Moffusilite,* the local news sheet, carried very little news of the disturbances. The army officers made their rounds without noticing anything unusual, and the civilians went to their offices. In the evening they met in the usual fashion, to eat and drink and dance.

On the 30th of May it was Dr Bowling's turn as host. In his drawing-room, young Lieutenant Scott strummed a guitar, while Mrs Bowling sang a romantic ballad. Four army officers sat down to a game of whist, while Mrs Ricketts, Mr Jenkins, the Collector, and Captain James, discussed the weather over a bottle of Exshaw's whisky.

Only the Labadoors had any foreboding of trouble. They were not at the party.

Mr Labadoor was 42, his wife 38. Their daughter, Ruth, was a pretty girl, with raven black hair and dark, lustrous eyes. She had left Mrs Shield's school at Fatehgarh only a fortnight before, because her mother felt she would be safer at home.

Mrs Labadoor's father had been a French adventurer who had served in the Maratha army; her mother came from a well-known Muslim family of Rampur. Her name was Mariam: she and her brothers had been brought up as Christians. At eighteen, she married Labadoor, a quiet, unassuming man, who was a clerk in the magistrate's office. He was a grandson of a merchant from Jersey (in the Channel Islands), and his original Jersey name was Labadu.

While most of the British wives in the cantonment thought it beneath their dignity to gossip with servants, Mariam Labadoor, who made few social calls, enjoyed these conversations of hers. Often they enlivened her day by reporting the juiciest scandals, on which they were always well-informed. But from what Mariam had heard recently, she was convinced that it was only a matter of hours before rioting broke out in the city. News of the events at Meerut had reached the bazaars and sepoy lines, and a fakir, who lived near the River Khannaut, was said to have predicted the end of the English East India Company's rule in the coming months. Mariam made her husband and daughter stay at home the evening of the Bowling's party, and had even suggested that they avoid going to church the next day, Sunday: a surprising request from Mariam, a regular church-goer.

Ruth liked having her way, and insisted on going to church the next day; and her father promised to accompany her.

The sun rose in a cloudless, shimmering sky, and only those who had risen at dawn had been lucky enough to enjoy the cool breeze that had blown across the river for a brief spell. At seven o'clock the church bell began to toll, and people could be seen making their way towards the small, sturdily built cantonment church. Some, like Mr Labadoor and his daughter, were on foot, wearing their Sunday clothes. Others came in carriages, or were borne aloft in *doolies* manned by sweating *doolie*-bearers.

St Mary's, the little church in Shahjahanpur, is situated on the southern boundary of the cantonment, near an ancient mango-grove. There are three entrances: one to the south, facing a large compound known as Buller's; another to the west, below the steeple; and the vestry door opening to the north. A narrow staircase leads up to the steeple. To the east there were open fields sloping down to the river, cultivated with melon; to the west, lay an open plain bounded by the city ; while the parade ground stretched away to the north until it reached the barracks of the sepoys. The bungalows scattered about the side of the parade ground belonged to the regimental officers, Englishmen who had slept soundly, quite unaware of an atmosphere charged with violence.

I will let Ruth take up the story . . . .

At The Church

Father and I had just left the house when we saw several sepoys crossing the road, on their way to the river for their morning bath. They stared so fiercely at us that I pressed close to my father and whispered, 'Papa, how strange they look!' But their appearance did not strike him as unusual: the sepoys usually passed that way when going to the River Khannaut, and I suppose Father was used to meeting them on his way to office.

We entered the church from the south porch, and took our seats in the last pew to the right. A number of people had already arrived, but I did not particularly notice who they were. We had knelt down, and were in the middle of the Confession, when we heared a tumult outside and a lot of shouting, that seemed nearer every moment. Everyone in the church got up, and Father left our pew and went and stood at the door, where I joined him.

There were six or seven men on the porch. Their faces were covered up to their noses, and they wore tight loincloths as though they had prepared for a wrestling bout; but they held naked swords in their hands. As soon as they saw us, they sprang forward, and one of them made a cut at us. The sword missed us both and caught the side of the door where it buried itself in the wood. My father had his left hand against the door, and I rushed out from under it, and escaped into the church compound.

A second and third cut were made at my father by the others, both of which caught him on his right cheek. Father tried to seize the sword of one of his assailants, but he caught it high up on the blade, and so firmly, that he lost two fingers from his right hand. These were the only cuts he received; but though he did not fall, he was bleeding profusely. All this time I had stood looking on from the porch, completely bewildered and dazed by what had happened. I remember asking my father what had happened to make him bleed so much.

'Take the handkerchief from my pocket and bandage my face,' he said.

When I had made a bandage from both our handkerchiefs and

tied it about his head, he said he wished to go home. I took him by the hand and tried to lead him out of the porch; but we had gone only a few steps when he began to feel faint, and said, 'I can't walk, Ruth. Let us go back to the church.'

The armed men had made only one rush through the church, and had then gone off through the vestry door. After wounding my father, they had run up the centre of the aisle, slashing right and left. They had taken a cut at Lieutenant Scott, but his mother threw herself over him and received the blow on her ribs; her tight clothes saved her from a serious injury. Mr Ricketts, Mr Jenkins, the Collector, and Mr MacCullam, the Minister, ran out through the vestry.

The rest of the congregation had climbed up to the belfry, and on my father's urging me to do so, I joined them there. We saw Captain James riding up to the church, quite unaware of what was happening. We shouted him a warning, but as he looked up at us, one of the sepoys, who were scattered about on the parade ground, fired at him, and he fell from his horse. Now two other officers came running from the Mess, calling out to the sepoys: 'Oh! children, what are you doing?' They tried to pacify their men, but no one listened to them. They had, however, been popular officers with the sepoys, who did not prevent them from joining us in the turret with their pistols in their hands.

Just then we saw a carriage coming at full speed towards the church. It was Dr Bowling's, and it carried him, his wife and child, and the nanny. The carriage had to cross the parade ground, and they were halfway across, when a bullet hit the doctor who was sitting on the coach box. He doubled up in his seat, but did not let go of the reins, and the carriage had almost reached the church, when a sepoy ran up and made a slash at Mrs Bowling, missing her by inches. When the carriage reached the church, some of the officers ran down to help Dr Bowling off the coach box. He struggled in their arms for a while, and was dead when they got him to the ground.

I had come down from the turret with the officers, and now ran to where my father lay. He was sitting against the wall, in a large pool of blood. He did not complain of any pain, but his lips were parched, and he kept his eyes open with an effort. He told me to go home, and to ask Mother to send someone with a cot, or a *doolie,* to carry him back. So much had happened so quickly that I was completely dazed, and though Mrs Bowling and the other women were weeping, there wasn't a tear in my eye. There were two great wounds on my father's face, and I was reluctant to leave him, but to run home and fetch a *doolie* seemed to be the only way in which I could help him.

Leaving him against the stone wall of the church, I ran round to the vestry side and almost fell over Mr Ricketts, who was lying about twelve feet from the vestry door. He had been attacked by an expert and powerful swordsman, whose blow had cut through the trunk from the left shoulder separating the head and right hand from the rest of the body. Sick with horror, I turned from the spot and began running home through Buller's compound.

Nobody met me on the way. No one challenged me, or tried to intercept or molest me. The cantonment seemed empty and deserted; but just as I reached the end of Buller's compound, I saw our house in flames. I stopped at the gate, looking about for my mother, but could not see her anywhere. Granny, too, was missing, and the servants. Then I saw Lala Ramjimal walking down the road towards me.

'Don't worry, my child,' he said. 'Mother, Granny and the others are all safe. Come, I will take you to them.'

There was no question of doubting Lala Ramjimal's intentions. He had held me on his knee when I was a baby, and I had grown up under his eyes. He led me to a hut some thirty yards from our old home. It was a mud house, facing the road, and its door was closed. Lala knocked on the door, but received no answer; then he put his mouth to a chink and whispered, '*Missy-baba* is with me, open the door.'

The door opened, and I rushed into my mother's arms.

'Thank God!' she cried. 'At least one is spared to me.'

'Papa is wounded at the church,' I said. 'Send someone to fetch him.'

Mother looked up at Lala and he could not resist the appeal in her eyes.

'I will go,' he said. 'Do not move from here until I return.'

'You don't know where he is,' I said. 'Let me come with you and help you.'

'No, you must not leave your mother now,' said Lala. 'If you are seen with me, we shall both be killed.'

He returned in the afternoon, after several hours. 'Sahib is dead,' he said, very simply. 'I arrived in time to see him die. He had lost so much blood that it was impossible for him to live. He could not speak, and his eyes were becoming glazed, but he looked at me in such a way that I am sure he recognized me . . . .'

Lala Ramjimal

Lala left us in the afternoon, promising to return when it grew dark, then he would take us to his own house. He ran a grave risk in doing so, but he had promised us his protection, and he was a man who, once he had decided on taking a certain course of action, could not be shaken from his purpose. He was not a Government servant and owed no loyalties to the British; nor had he conspired with the rebels, for his path never crossed theirs. He had been content always to go about his business (he owned several *doolies* and carriages, which he hired out to Europeans who could not buy their own) in a quiet and efficient manner, and was held in some respect by those he came into contact with; his motives were always personal, and if he helped us, it was not because we belonged to the ruling class—my father was probably the most junior officer in Shahjahanpur—but because he had known us for many years, and had grown fond of my mother, who had always treated him as a friend and equal.

I realized that I was now fatherless, and my mother, a widow; but we had no time to indulge in our private sorrow. Our own lives were in constant danger. From our hiding place we could hear the crackling of timber coming from our burning house. The road from the city to the cantonment was in an uproar, with people shouting on all sides. We heard the tramp of men passing up and down the road, just in front of our door; a moan or a sneeze would have betrayed us, and then we would have been at the mercy of the most ruffianly elements from the bazaar, whose swords flashed in the dazzling sunlight.

There were eight of us in the little room: Mother, Granny, myself; my cousin, Anet; my mother's half-brother, Pilloo, who was about my age, and his mother; our servants, Champa and Lado; as well as two of our black and white spaniels, who had followed close on Mother's heels when she fled from the house.

The mud hut in which we were sheltering was owned by Tirloki, a mason who had helped build our own house. He was well-known to us. Weeks before the outbreak, when Mother used to gossip with her servants and others about the possibility of trouble in Shahjahanpur, Tirloki had been one of those who had offered his house for shelter should she ever be in need of it. And Mother, as a precaution, had accepted his offer, and taken the key from him.

Mother afterwards told me that, as she sat on the veranda that morning, one of the gardener's sons had come running to her in great haste, and had cried out: 'Mutiny broken out, Sahib and *Missy-baba* killed!' Hearing that we had both been killed, Mother's first impulse was to throw herself into the nearest well; but Granny caught hold of her, and begged her not to be rash, saying, 'And what will become of the rest of us if you do such a thing?' And so she had gone across the road, followed by the others, and had entered Tirloki's house and chained the door from within.

We were shut up in the hut all day, expecting, at any moment, to be discovered and killed. We had no food at all, but we could not have eaten any had it been there. My father gone, our future appeared a perfect void, and we found it difficult to talk. A hot wind blew through the cracks in the door, and our throats were parched. Late in the afternoon, a *chatty* of cold water was let down to us from a tree outside a window at the rear of the hut. This was an act of compassion on the part of a man called Chinta, who had worked for us as a labourer when our bungalow was being built.

At about ten o'clock, Lala returned, accompanied by Dhani, our old bearer. He proposed to take us to his own house. Mother hesitated to come out into the open, but Lala assured her that the roads were quite clear now, and there was little fear of our being molested. At last, she agreed to go.

We formed two batches. Lala led the way with a drawn sword in one hand, his umbrella in the other. Mother and Anet and I followed, holding each other's hands. Mother had thrown over us a counterpane which she had been carrying with her when she left the house. We avoided the main road, making our way round the sweeper settlement, and reached Lala's house after a fifteen-minute walk. On our arrival there, Lala offered us a bed to sit upon, while he squatted down on the ground with his legs crossed.

Mother had thrown away her big bunch of keys as we left Tirloki's house. When I asked her why she had done so, she pointed to the smouldering ruins of our bungalow and said: 'Of what possible use could they be to us now?'

The bearer, Dhani, arrived with the second batch, consisting of dear Granny, Pilloo and his mother, and Champa and Lado, and the dogs. There we were, eight of us in Lala's small house; and, as far as I could tell, his own family was as large as ours.

We were offered food, but we could not eat. We lay down for the night—Mother, Granny and I on the bed, the rest on the ground. And in the darkness, with my face against my mother's bosom, I gave vent to my grief and wept bitterly. My mother wept, too, but silently, and I think she was still weeping when at last I fell asleep.

In Lala's House

Lala Ramjimal's family consisted of himself, his wife, mother, aunt and sister. It was a house of women, and our unexpected arrival hadn't changed that. It must indeed have been a test of Lala's strength and patience, with twelve near-hysterical females on his hands!

His family, of course, knew who we were, because Lala's mother and aunt used to come and draw water from our well, and offer *bél* leaves at the little shrine near our house. They were at first shy of us; and we, so immersed in our own predicament, herded together in a corner of the house, and looked at each other's faces, and wept. Lala's wife would come and serve us food in platters made of stitched leaves. We ate once in twenty-four hours, a little after noon, but we were satisfied with this one big meal.

The house was an ordinary mud building, consisting of four flat-roofed rooms, with a low veranda in the front, and a courtyard at the back. It was small and unpretentious, occupied by a family of small means.

Lala's wife was a young woman, short in stature, with a fair complexion. We didn't know her name, because it is not customary for a husband or wife to call the other by name; but her mother-in-law would address her as *Dulhan,* or bride.

Ramjimal himself was a tall, lean man, with long mustachios. His speech was always very polite, like that of most Kayasthas but he had an air of determination about him that was rare in others.

On the second day of our arrival, I overheard his mother speaking to him: 'Lalaji, you have made a great mistake in bringing these *Angrezans* into our house. What will people say? As soon as the rebels hear of it, they will come and kill us.'

'I have done what is right,' replied Lala very quietly. 'I have not given shelter to *Angrezans*. I have given shelter to friends. Let people say or think as they please.'

He seldom went out of the house, and was usually to be seen seated before the front door, either smoking his small hookah, or playing chess with some friend who happened to drop by. After a few days, people began to suspect that there was somebody in the house about whom Lala was being very discreet, but they had no idea who these guests could be. He kept a close watch on his family, to prevent them from talking too much; and he saw that no one entered the house, keeping the front door chained at all times.

It is a wonder that we were able to live undiscovered for as long as we did, for there were always the dogs to draw attention to the house. They would not leave us, though we had nothing to offer them except the leftovers from our own meals. Lala's aunt told Mother that the third of our dogs, who had not followed us, had been seen going round and round the smoking ruins of our bungalow, and that on the day after the outbreak, he was found dead, sitting up—waiting for his master's return!

One day, Lala came in while we were seated on the floor talking about the recent events. Anxiety for the morrow had taken the edge off our grief, and we were able to speak of what had happened without becoming hysterical.

Lala sat down on the ground with a foil in his hand—the weapon had become his inseparable companion, but I do not think he had yet had occasion to use it. It was not his own, but one that he had found on the floor of the looted and ransacked courthouse.

'Do you think we are safe in your house, Lala?' asked Mother. 'What is going on outside these days?'

'You are quite safe here,' said Lala, gesturing with the foil. 'No one comes into this house except over my dead body. It is true, though, that I am suspected of harbouring kafirs. More than one person has asked me why I keep such a close watch over my house. My reply is, that as the outbreak has put me out of employment, what would they have me do except sit in front of my house and look after my women? Then they ask me why I have not been to the Nawab, like everyone else.'

'What Nawab, Lala?' asked Mother.

'After the sepoys entered the city, their leader, the Subedar-Major, set up Qadar Ali Khan as the Nawab, and proclaimed it throughout the city. Nizam Ali, a pensioner, was made Kotwal, and responsible posts were offered to Javed Khan, and to Nizam Ali Khan, but the latter refused to accept office.'

'And the former?'

'He has taken no office yet, because he and Azzu Khan have been too busy plundering the sahibs' houses. Javed Khan also instigated an attack on the treasurer. It was like this . . . .

'Javed Khan, as you know, is one of the biggest ruffians in the city. When the sepoys had returned to their lines after proclaiming the Nawab, Javed Khan paid a visit to their commander. On learning that the regiment was preparing to leave Shahjahanpur and join the Bareilly brigade, he persuaded the Subedar-Major, Ghansham Singh, to make a raid on the Rosa Rum Factory before leaving. A detachment, under Subedar Zorawar Singh, accompanied Javed Khan, and they took the road which passes by Jhunna Lal, the treasurer's house. There they halted, and demanded a contribution from Jhunna Lal. It so happened that he had only that morning received a sum of six thousand rupees from the Tehsildar of Jalalabad, and this the Subedar seized at once. As Jhunna Lal refused to part with any more, he was tied hand and foot and suspended from a tree by his legs. At the same time Javed Khan seized all his account books and threw them into a well, saying, "Since you won't give us what we need, there go your accounts! We won't leave you with the means of collecting money from others!"

'After the party had moved on, Jhunna Lal's servants took him down from the tree. He was half-dead with fright, and from the rush of blood to his head. But when he came to himself, he got his servants to go down the well and fish up every account book!'

'And what about the Rosa Factory?' I asked.

'Javed Khan's party set fire to it, and no less than 70,000 gallons of rum, together with a large quantity of loaf sugar, were destroyed. The rest was carried away. Javed Khan's share of loaf sugar was an entire cart-load!'*

The next day when Lala came in and sat beside us—he used to spend at least an hour in our company every day—I asked him a question that had been on my mind much of the time, but the answer to which I was afraid of hearing: the whereabouts of my father's body.

'I would have told you before, *Missy-baba*,' he said, 'but I was afraid of upsetting you. The day after I brought you to my house I went again to the church, and there I found the body of your father, of the Collector-Sahib, and the doctor, exactly where I had seen them the day before. In spite of their exposure and the great heat they had not decomposed at all, and neither the vultures nor the jackals had touched them. Only their shoes had gone.

'As I turned to leave I saw two persons, Muslims, bringing in the body of Captain James, who had been shot at a little distance from the church. They laid it beside that of your father and Dr Bowling. They told me that they had decided to bury the mortal remains of those Christians who had been killed. I told them that they were taking a risk in doing so, as they might be accused by the Nawab's men of being in sympathy with the Firangis. They replied that they were aware of the risk, but that something had impelled them to undertake this task, and that they were willing to face the consequences.

'I was put to shame by their intentions, and, removing my long coat, began to help them carry the bodies to a pit they had dug outside the church. Here I saw, and was able to identify, the bodies of Mr MacCullam, the *Padri*-Sahib, and Mr Smith, the Assistant Collector. All six were buried side-by-side, and we covered the grave with a masonry slab upon which we drew parallel lines to mark each separate grave. We finished the work within an hour, and when I left the place I felt a satisfaction which I cannot describe . . . .'

Later, when we had recovered from the emotions which Ramjimal's words had aroused in us, I asked him how Mr MacCullam, the chaplain, had met his death; for I remembered seeing him descending from his pulpit when the ruffians entered the church, and running

* The Rosa Rum Factory recovered, and survives to this day.

through the vestry with Mr Ricketts' mother.

'I cannot tell you much,' said Lala. 'I only know that while the sepoys attacked Mr Ricketts, Mr MacCullam was able to reach the melon field and conceal himself under some creepers. But another gang found him there, and finished him off with their swords.'

'Poor Mr MacCullam!' sighed Mother. 'He was such a harmless little man. And what about Arthur Smith, Lala?' Mother was determined to find out what had happened to most of the people we had known.

'Assistant-Sahib was murdered in the city,' said Lala. 'He was in his bungalow, ill with fever, when the trouble broke out. His idea was to avoid the cantonment and make for the city, thinking it was only the sepoys who had mutinied. He went to the courts, but found them a shambles, and while he was standing in the street, a mob collected round him and began to push him about. Somebody prodded him with the hilt of his sword. Mr Smith lost his temper and, in spite of his fever, drew his revolver and shot at the man. But alas for Smith-Sahib, the cap snapped and the charge refused to explode. He levelled again at the man, but this time the bullet had no effect, merely striking the metal clasp of the man's belt and falling harmlessly to the ground. Mr Smith flung away his revolver in disgust, and now the man cut at him with his sword and brought him to his knees. Then the mob set upon him. Fate was against Smith-Sahib. The Company Bahadur's prestige has gone, for who ever heard of a revolver snapping, or a bullet being resisted by a belt?'

A Change of Name

According to the reports we received from Lala Ramjimal, it seemed that by the middle of June every European of Shahjahanpur had been killed—if not in the city, then at Muhamdi, across the Khannaut, where many, including Mrs Bowling and her child, had fled. The only survivors were ourselves and (as we discovered later), the Redmans. And we had survived only because the outer world believed that we too, had perished. This was made clear to us one day when a woman came to the door to sell fish.

Lala's wife remarked: 'You have come after such a long time.

And you don't seem to have sold anything today ?'

'Ah, Lalain!' said the woman. 'Who is there to buy from me? The Firangis are gone. There was a time when I used to be at the Labadoor house every day, and I never went away without making four or five annas. Not only did the memsahib buy from me, but sometimes she used to get me to cook the fish for her, for which she used to pay me an extra two annas.'

'And what has become of them?' asked Lalain.

'Why, the sahib and his daughter were killed in the church, while the memsahib went and threw herself in the river.'

'Are you sure of this?' asked Lalain.

'Of course!' said the woman. 'My husband, while fishing next morning, saw her body floating down the Khannaut!'

We had been in Lala Ramjimal's house for two weeks, and our clothes had become dirty and torn. There had been no time to bring any clothing with us, and there was no possibility of changing, unless we adopted Indian dress. And so Mother borrowed a couple of petticoats and light shawls from Lalain, and altered them to our measurements. We had to wash them in the courtyard whenever they became dirty, and stand around wrapped in sheets until they were half-dry.

Mother also considered it prudent to take Indian names. I was given the name of Khurshid, which is Persian for 'Sun', and my cousin Anet, being short of stature, was called Nanni. Pilloo was named Ghulam Husain, and his mother automatically became known as Ghulam Husain's mother. Granny was of course, Bari-Bi. It was easier for us to take Mohammedan names, because we were fluent in Urdu, and because Granny did in fact come from a Muslim family of Rampur. We soon fell into the habits of Lala's household, and it would have been very difficult for anyone, who had known us before, to recognize us as the Labadoors.

Life in Lala's house was not without its touches of humour. There lived with us a woman named Ratna, wife to Imrat Lal, a relative of Lala's. He was a short, stout man. She was tall, and considered ugly. He had no children by her, and after some time, had become intimate with a low-caste woman, who used to fill water for his family and was, like himself, short and stout. He had two sons by her, and though his longing for children was now satisfied, his peace of mind was soon disturbed by the wranglings of his two wives. He was an astrologer by profession; and, one day, after consulting the stars, he made up his mind to desert his family and seek his fortune elsewhere. His wives, left to themselves, now made up their differences and began to live together. The first wife earned a living as a seamstress, the second used to grind. Occasionally, there would be outbreaks of jealousy. The second wife would taunt the first for being barren, and the seamstress would reply, 'When you drew water, you had corns on your hands and feet. Now grinding has given you corns on your fingers. Where next are you going to get corns?'

Imrat Lal had meanwhile, become a yogi and soothsayer, and began to make a comfortable living in Haridwar. Having heard of his whereabouts, the second wife had a petition writer draw up a letter for her, which she asked me to read to her, as I knew Urdu. It went something like this:

'Oh thou who hast vanished like mustard oil which, when absorbed by the skin, leaves only its odour behind; thou with the rotund form dancing before my eyes, and the owl's eyes which were wont to stare at me vacantly; wilt thou still snap thy fingers at me when this letter is evidence of my unceasing thought of thee? Why did you call me your *lado*, your loved one, when you had no love for me? And why have you left me to the taunts of that stick of a woman whom you in your perversity used to call a precious stone, your Ratna? Who has proved untrue, you or I? Why have you sported thus with my feelings? Drown yourself in a handful of water, or return and make my hated rival an ornament for your neck, or wear her effigy nine times round your arm as a charm against my longings for you.'

But she received no reply to this letter. Probably when Imrat Lal read it, he consulted the stars again, and decided it was best to move further on into the hills, leaving his family to the care of his generous relative, Lala Ramjimal.

As the hot weather was now at its height, everyone slept out in the courtyard, including Lala and the female members of his household. We had become one vast family. Everyone slept well, except mother, who, though she rested during the day, stayed awake all night, watching over us. It was distressing to see her sit up night after night, determined not to fall asleep. Her forebodings of danger were as strong as before. Lala would fold his hands to her and say, 'Do sleep, Mariam. I am no Mathur if I shirk my duty.' But her only reply was to ask him for a knife that she could keep beside her. He gave her a rusty old knife, and she took great pains to clean it and sharpen its edges.

A day came when mother threatened to use it.

It was ten o'clock and everyone had gone to bed, except Mother, who still sat at the foot of my cot. I was just dozing off, when she remarked that she could get the smell of jasmine flowers, which was strange, because there was no jasmine bush near the house. At the same time, a clod of earth fell from the high wall, and looking up, we saw in the dark, the figure of a man stretched across it. There was another man a little further along, concealed in the shadows of a neem tree that grew at the end of the yard. Mother drew her knife from beneath her pillow, and called out that she would pierce the heart of the first man who attempted to lay his hands on us. Impressed by her ferocity, which was like that of a tigress guarding its young, the intruders quietly disappeared into the night.

This incident led us to believe that we were still unsafe, and that our existence was known to others. A few days later, something else happened that made us even more nervous.

Lado, one of the two servants who had followed us, had been permitted by Lala to occupy a corner of the house. She had a daughter married to a local sword-cleaner, who had been going about looking for Lado ever since the outbreak. Hearing the rumour that there were Firangis hiding in Lala's house, he appeared at the front door on the 23rd of June, and spoke to Lala.

'I am told that my mother-in-law is here,' he said. 'I have enquired everywhere, and people tell me that she was seen to come only as far as this. So, Lalaji, you had better let me take her away, or I shall bring trouble upon you.'

Lala denied any knowledge of Lado's whereabouts, but the man was persistent, and asked to be allowed to search the house.

'You will do no such thing,' said Ramjimal. 'Go your way, insolent fellow. How dare you propose to enter my zenana?'

The man left in a huff, threatening to inform the Nawab, and to bring some sepoys to the house. When Lado heard of what had happened, she came into the room and fell down at Mother's feet, insisting that she leave immediately, lest her son-in-law brought us any trouble. She blessed me and my cousin, and left the house in tears. Poor Lado! She had been with us many years, and we had all come to like her. She had touched our hearts with her loyalty during our troubles.

In the evening, when Lala came home, he told us of what had befallen Lado. She had met her son-in-law in the city.

'Where have you been, Mother?' He had said. 'I have been searching for you everywhere. From where have you suddenly sprung up?'

'I am just returning from Fatehgarh,' she said.

'Why, Mother, what took you to Fatehgarh? And what has become of the *Angrezans* you were serving?'

'Now, how am I to know what became of them?' replied Lado. 'They were all killed, I suppose. Someone saw Labadoor-Mem drowned in the Khannaut.'

The Nawab heard of the sudden reappearance of our old servant, and sending for her, had her closely questioned; but Lado maintained that she did not know what had happened to us.

The Nawab swore at her. 'This 'dead one' tries to bandy words with me,' he said. 'She knows where they are, but will not tell. On my oath, I will have your head chopped off, unless you tell me everything you know about them. Do you hear?'

'My lord!' answered Lado, trembling from head to foot. 'How can I tell you what I do not know myself? True, I fled with them from the burning house, but where they went afterwards, I do not know.'

'This she-devil!' swore the Nawab. 'She will be the cause of my committing a violent act. She evades the truth. All right, let her be dealt with according to her desserts.'

Two men rushed up, and, seizing Lado by the hair, held a naked sword across her throat. The poor woman writhed and wriggled in the grasp of her captors, protesting her innocence and begging for mercy.

'I swear by your head, my lord, that I know nothing.'

'So you swear by my head, too?' raged the Nawab. 'Well, since you are not afraid even of the sword, I suppose you know nothing. Let her go.'

And poor Lado, half-dead through fright, was released and sent on her way.

Another Nawab

On the 24th of June there was a great beating of drums, and in the distance we heard the sound of fife and drum. We hadn't heard these familiar sounds since the day of the outbreak, and now we wondered what could be happening. There was much shouting on the road, and the trample of horses, and we waited impatiently for Lala to come home and satisfy our curiosity.

'A change of Nawabs today?' enquired Mother. 'How will it affect us?'

'It isn't possible to say as yet. Ghulam Qadar Khan is the same sort of man as his predecessor, and they come from the same family. Both of them were opposed to the Company's rule. There is this difference, though: whereas Qadar Ali was a dissolute character and ineffective in many ways, Ghulam Qadar has energy, and is said to be pious—but he, too, has expressed his determination to rid this land of all Firangis . . . .

'When the Mutiny first broke out, he was in Oudh, where he had been inciting the rural population to throw off the foreign yoke. He would have acted in unison with Qadar Ali had they not already disagreed; for Ghulam Qadar was against the murder of women and children. However, Qadar Ali's counsels prevailed, and Ghulam Qadar withdrew for a while, to watch the course of events. Now several powerful landholders have thrown their lot in with him, including Nizam Ali Khan, Vittal Singh, Abdul Rauf, and even that ruffian, Javed Khan. Yesterday, he entered Shahjahanpur, and without any opposition, took over the government. This morning the leading rebels attended the durbar of the new Nawab. And tonight the Nawab holds an entertainment.'

'Do you think he will trouble us, Lala?' asked Granny anxiously. 'What has he to gain by killing such harmless people as us?'

'I cannot say anything for certain, Bari-Bi,' said Lala. 'He might wish to popularize his reign by exterminating a few kafirs as his predecessor did. But there is a rumour in the city that he has been afflicted with some deep sorrow . . . .'

'What could it be?' asked Mother. 'Is his wife dead? Surely he can get another, especially now that he is the Nawab. And how can his grief affect us?'

'It could influence his actions,' said Lala. 'The rumour is that his daughter Zinat, a young and beautiful girl, has been abducted by a lover. Where she has been taken, no one knows.'

'And the lover?' asked Mother, displaying for a moment her habitual curiosity about other people's romantic affairs.

'They say that Farhat, one of Qadar Ali's sons, disappeared at the same time. They suspect that he has eloped with the girl.'

'Ah, I remember Farhat,' said Mother. 'A handsome young fellow who often passed in front of our house, showing off on a piebald nag. Still, what has all this to do with us?'

'I was coming to that, Mariam,' said Lala. 'No sooner had the Nawab taken his seat at the durbar, than some informers came to him with the story about Lado, and suggested that my house be searched for your family, who they believed were in hiding here. Well, the Nawab wanted to know what had happened to Labadoor-Sahib who, he remarked, had always been a harmless and inoffensive man. When told that he had been killed along with the others in the church, the Nawab said, "So be it. Then we need not go out of our way to look for his women. I will have nothing to do with the murder of the innocent . . . ." '

'How far can we trust his present mood?' asked Mother.

'I was told by Nizam Ali Khan that the Nawab once gave his daughter a certain promise—that he would not lift his hand against the women and children of the Firangis. It sounds very unlikely, I know. But I think Nizam Ali's information is usually reliable.'

'That is true,' said Mother. 'My husband knew him well. We had the lease of his compound for several years, and we paid the rent regularly.'

'Well, the Nawab likes him,' said Lala. 'He has given him orders to begin casting guns in his private armoury. If the Nawab sticks to men like Nizam Ali, public affairs will be handled more efficiently than they would have been under Qadar Ali Khan.'

We had all along been dependent upon Lala Ramjimal for our daily necessities, and though Mother had a little money in her jewel box, which she had brought with her, she had to use it very sparingly.

One day, folding his hands before her, Lala said, 'Mariam, I am ashamed to say it, but I have no money left. Business has been at a standstill, and the little money I had saved is all but finished.'

'Don't be upset, Lala,' said Mother, taking some leaf-gold from her jewel box and giving it to him. 'Take this gold to the bazaar, and sell it for whatever you can get.'

Lala was touched, and at the same time, overjoyed, at this unexpected help.

'I shall go to the bazaar immediately, and see what I can get for it,' he said. 'And I have a suggestion, Mariam. Let us all go to Bareilly. I have my brother there, and some of your relatives are also there. We shall at least save on house rent, which I am paying here. If you agree, I will hire two carts which should accomodate all of us.'

We readily agreed to Lala's suggestion, and he walked off happily to the bazaar, unaware that his plans for our safety were shortly to go awry.

Caught!

We had been with Lala almost a month, and this was to be our last day in his house.

We were, as usual, huddled together in one room, discussing our future prospects, when our attention was drawn to the sound of men's voices outside.

'Open the door!' shouted someone, and there was a loud banging on the front door.

We did not answer the summons, but cast nervous glances at each other. Lalain, who had been sitting with us, got up and left the room, and chained our door from the other side.

'Open up or we'll force your door in!' demanded the voice outside, and the banging now became more violent.

Finally, Ratna went to the front door and opened it, letting in some twenty to thirty men, all armed with swords and pistols. One of them, who had done all the shouting and seemed to be the leader, ordered the women to go up to the roof of the house, as he intended searching all the rooms for the fugitive Firangis. Lala's family had no alternative but to obey him, and they went up to the roof. The men now approached the door of our room, and we heard the wrench of the chain as it was drawn out. The leader, pushing the door open violently, entered the room with a naked sword in his hand.

'Where is Labadoor's daughter?' he demanded of mother, gripping her by the arm and looking intently into her face. 'No, this is not her,' he said, dropping her hand and turning to look at me.

'This is the girl!' he exclaimed, taking me by the hand and dragging me away from Mother, into the light of the courtyard. He held his uplifted sword in his right hand.

'No!' cried Mother, in a tone of anguish, throwing herself in front of me. 'If you would take my daughter's life, take mine before hers, I beg of you by the sword of Ali!'

Her eyes were bloodshot, starting out of their sockets, and she presented a magnificent, and quite terrifying sight. I think she frightened me even more than the man with the raised sword; but I clung to her instinctively, and tried to wrest my arm from the man's grasp. But so impressed was he by Mother's display, that he dropped the point of his sword, and in a gruff voice commanded us both to follow him quietly, if we valued our lives. Granny sat wringing her hands in desperation, while the others remained huddled together in a corner, concealing Pilloo, the only boy, beneath their shawls. The man with the sword led Mother and me from the house, followed by his band of henchmen.

It was the end of June, and the monsoon rains had not yet arrived. It was getting on for noon, and the sun beat down mercilessly. The ground was hard and dry and dusty. Barefooted and bareheaded, we followed our captor without a murmur, like lambs going to slaughter. The others hemmed us in, all with drawn swords, their steel blades glistening in the sun. We had no idea where we were being taken, or what was in store for us.

After walking half a mile, during which our feet were blistered on the hot surface of the road, our captor halted under a tamarind tree, near a small mosque, and told us to rest. We told him we were thirsty, and some water was brought to us in a brass jug. A crowd of curious people had gathered around us.

'These are the Firangans who were hiding with the Lala! How miserable they look. But one is young—she has fine eyes! They are her mother's eyes—notice!'

A pir, a wandering hermit, who was in the group, touched our captor on the shoulder and said, 'Javed, you have taken away these unfortunates to amuse yourself. Give me your word of honour that you will not illtreat or kill them.'

'So this is Javed Khan,' whispered Mother.

Javed Khan, his face still muffled, brought his sword to a slant before his face. 'I swear by my sword that I will neither kill nor illtreat them!'

'Take care for your soul, Javed,' said the pir. 'You have taken an oath which no Pathan would break and still expect to survive. Let no harm come to these two, or you may expect a short lease of life!'

'Have no fear for that!' said Javed Khan, signalling us to rise.

We followed him as before, leaving the crowd of gazers behind, and taking the road that led into the narrow mohalla of Jalalnagar, the Pathan quarter of the city.

Passing down several lanes, we arrived at a small square, at one end of which a horse was tied. Javed Khan slapped the horse on the rump, and opening the door of his house, told us to enter. He came in behind us. In the courtyard, we saw a young woman sitting on a swing. She seemed astonished to see us.

'These are the Firangans,' said Javed Khan, closing the front door behind him and walking unconcernedly across the courtyard.

An elderly woman approached Mother.

'Don't be afraid,' she said. 'Sit down and rest a little.'

Javed Khan

When Javed Khan returned to his zenana after a wash and a change of clothes, he addressed his wife.

'What do you think of my Firangans? Didn't I say I would not rest until I found them? A lesser man would have given up the search long ago!' And chuckling, he sat down to his breakfast, which was served to him on a low, wooden platform.

His aunt, the elderly woman who had first welcomed us, and who was known as Kothiwali, spoke gently to Mother.

'Tell me,' she said, 'tell me something of your story. Who are you?'

'You see us for what we are,' replied Mother. 'Dependent on others, at the mercy of your relative who may kill us whenever it takes his fancy.'

'Who is going to take your miserable lives?' interrupted Javed Khan.

'No, you are safe while I am here,' said Kothiwali. 'You may speak to me without fear. What is your name, and that of the girl with you?'

'The girl is Khurshid, my only daughter. My name is Mariam, and my family is well-known in Rampur, where my father was a minister to the Nawab.'

'Which Rampur?' asked Khan-Begum, Javed's wife.

'*Rohelon-ka-Rampur*,' replied Mother.

'Oh, *that* Rampur!' said Khan-Begum, evidently impressed by Mother's antecedents.

'This, my only child,' continued Mother, bestowing an affectionate glance at me, 'is the offspring of an Englishman. He was massacred in the church, on the day the outbreak took place. So I am now a widow, and the child, fatherless. Our lives were saved through the kindness of Lala Ramjimal, and we were living at his house until your relative took us away by force. My mother, and others of our family are still there. Only Allah knows what will become of us all, for there is no one left to protect us.'

Mother's feelings now overcame her, and she began weeping. This set me off too, and hiding my face in Mother's shawl, I began to sob.

Kothiwali was touched. She placed her hand on my head and said, 'Don't weep, child, don't weep,' in a sympathetic tone.

Mother wiped the tears from her eyes and looked up at the older woman. 'We are in great trouble, Pathani!' she said. 'Spare our lives and don't let us be dishonoured, I beg of you.'

Javed Khan, quite put out by all this weeping, now exclaimed, 'Put your mind at rest, good woman. No one will kill you, I can assure you. On the contrary, I have saved your daughter from dishonour at the hands of others. I intend to marry her honourably, whenever you will.'

The plate dropped from Javed Khan's wife's hand. He gave her a fierce look. 'Don't be such a fool, Qabil!' he said.

Before Mother could say anything, Kothiwali said, 'Javed, you should not have done this thing. These two are of good birth, and they are in distress. Look how faded and careworn they are! Be kind to them, I tell you, and do not insult them in their present condition.'

'Depend on it, *chachi*,' he replied. 'They will receive nothing but kindness from my hands. True, now they have fallen from their former greatness!'

'I should like to know how you became acquainted with them?' enquired Kothiwali. 'Is not your Khan-Begum as good a wife as any? Mark her fine nose!'

'Who says anything to the contrary? But, oh *chachi*!' he exclaimed. 'How can I make you understand the fascination this girl exerted over me when she was in her father's house! The very first time I saw her, I was struck by her beauty. She shone like Zohra, the morning star. Looking at her now, I realize the truth of the saying, that a flower never looks so beautiful as when it is on its parent stem. Break it, and it withers in the hand. Would anyone believe that this poor creature is the same angelic one I saw only a month ago?'

I was full of resentment, but could say nothing and do nothing, except press closer to my mother and look at Javed Khan with all the scorn I could muster. Khan-Begum, too, must have been seething with indignation; but she too was helpless, because Javed was well within his rights to think in terms of a second wife.

'The greater fool you, Javed, for depriving the child of her father, and breaking the flower from its stem before it had bloomed!' said Khan-Begum.

'What did you say, Qabil?' he asked sharply. 'No, don't repeat it again. The demon is only slumbering in my breast, and it will take little to rouse it.'

He gave me a scorching look, and I could not take my eyes from his face; I was like a doomed bird, fascinated by the gaze of a rattlesnake. But Mother was staring at him as though she would plumb his dark soul to its innermost depths, and he quailed under her stern gaze.

'Don't put me down for a common murderer,' he said apologetically. 'If I have taken lives, they have been those of infidels, enemies of my people. I am deserving of praise rather than blame.'

'Now don't excite yourself,' said Kothiwali, coming to the rescue again. 'What I wanted to bring home to you is that, if you are such an admirer of beauty, your Khan-Begum is neither ugly nor dark. I should have thought Firangi women had blue eyes and fair hair, but these poor things—how frightened they look!—would pass off as one of us!'

'All right, all right,' grumbled Javed Khan in a harsh voice.

'Don't carry on and on about Qabil's beauty, as if she ever possessed any. Let us drop the subject. But *chachi*,' and his eyes softened as he glanced at me, 'you should have judged this girl at the time I first set eyes on her. She was like a rose touched by a breath of wind, a doe-like creature . . . .'

'Will you not stop your rubbish?' interrupted Kothiwali. 'Look at her now, and tell me if she answers the same description.'

'*W'allah!* A change has come over them!' exclaimed Javed Khan wonderingly, and becoming poetical again. 'She is not what she used to be. Within a month she has aged twenty years. When I seized the girl by her arm at the Lala's house, she was ready to faint. But oh, how can I describe the terror which seized me at the sight of her mother! Like an enraged tigress, whose side has been pierced by a barbed arrow, she hurled herself at me, and presented her breast to my sword. I shall never forget the look she gave me as she thrust me away from the girl! I was awed. I was subdued. I was unmanned. The sword was ready to fall from my hand. Surely the blood of a hero runs in her veins! This is no ordinary female!' And bestowing a kindly glance on Mother, he exclaimed: 'A hundred mercies to thee, woman!'

Guests of the Pathan

I think you and I will be good friends,' said Kothiwali to Mother. 'I already love your daughter. Come, *beti*, come nearer to me,' she said, caressing my head.

Javed Khan had finished his meal and had gone out into the courtyard, leaving his wife and aunt alone to eat with us. Though we were hungry and thirsty, we did not have the heart to eat much with Granny's, and cousin Anet's, fate still unknown to us. But we took something, enough to keep up our strength, and when Javed Khan came in again, he seemed pleased that we had partaken of his food.

'Having tasted salt under my roof,' he said, 'you are no longer strangers in the house. You must make my house your home for the future.'

'It is very good of you to say so,' replied Mother. 'But there are others who are dependent on me, my mother and my niece, and without them, everything I eat, tastes bitter in my mouth.'

'Don't worry, they shall join you,' said Javed Khan. 'I had seen your daughter a long time before the outbreak, when I took a fancy to her. A ruffian had intended to carry her off before, and would have done so, had I not anticipated him. I have brought you here with the best of intentions. As soon as I have your consent, I propose to marry Khurshid, and will give her a wife's portion.'

'But how can you do that?' asked Mother. 'You have a wife already.'

'Well, what is there to prevent me having more wives than one? Our law allows it.'

'That may be,' rejoined Mother, 'but how can you, a Muslim, marry a Christian girl?'

'There is no reason why I may not,' replied Javed Khan. 'We Pathans can take a wife from any race or creed we please. And—' pausing as his wife let fall a petulant 'oh!' — 'I dare my wife to object to such a proceeding on my part. Did not my father take in a low-caste woman for her large, pretty eyes, the issue of that union being the brat, Saifullah—a plague on him!—and Kothiwali, whom you see here, was a low-caste Hindu, who charmed my uncle out of his wits. So what harm can there be if I take a Christian for a wife?'

My mother had a quiver full of counter arguments, but the time was not favourable for argument; it was safer to dissemble.

'I trust you will not expect an immediate answer to your request,' she said. 'I have just lost my husband, and there is no one to guide or advise me. Let us speak again on this subject at some other time.'

'I am in no hurry,' said Javed Khan. 'A matter of such importance cannot be settled in a day. Take a week, good woman. And do not forget that this is no sudden infatuation on my part. The girl has been in my mind for months. I am not Javed if I let the opportunity pass me by. Be easy in your mind—there is no hurry . . . .'

And he went out again into the courtyard.

All that had happened to us that morning, and Javed Khan's proposal of marriage, gave me food for thought for the rest of the day. A bed was put down for us in the veranda, and I lay down on my back, staring up at the ceiling where two small lizards darted about in search of flies. Mother was engrossed in a conversation with Kothiwali. Her perfect Urdu, her fine manners, and her high moral values, all took Kothiwali by storm. She was in raptures over Mother, and expressed every sympathy for us. She had come to Javed's house on a short visit, and did not feel like leaving.

'You must let Mariam come and spend a few days with me,' she said to her niece.

'And what is to become of her daughter?' replied Khan-Begum. 'Is she to be left here alone?'

'Of course not. She must come with her mother. And, Qabil, don't allow all this to upset you. Javed's head is a little befuddled nowadays, but he will be all right soon. As for these poor things, they are in no way to blame. You will come Mariam, won't you?'

'With pleasure,' said Mother. 'If we are allowed to.'

We were worrying about Granny and the others, when the sound of an altercation at the front door reached us. We recognized the voice of our friend and protector, Lala Ramjimal, who had tracked us down, and now insisted on seeing us.

'Khan Saheb!' we heard him say to Javed Khan. 'It was very wrong of you to enter my house during my absence, and to bring away my guests without my permission. Had I been there, you could only have done so by making your way over my dead body.'

'That is exactly why I came when you were not there,' replied Javed Khan. 'I had no wish to end your life.'

'I would not be a Mathur if I had not defended them. Well, what is done is done. I cannot force you to return them to my house. But let me be permitted to see if they need anything. I would also say goodbye to them.'

Mother went to the door and spoke to Lala, thanking him for taking the risk in coming to see us.

'What Vishnu ordered has come to pass,' said Lala resignedly. 'No skill of ours could have prevented it. But be comforted, for better days must lie ahead. I have brought your jewel box back for you.'

She took the jewel box from his hand, but did not bother to examine its contents, knowing that nothing would be missing.

'I have sold the gold you gave me,' said Lala, 'and I have brought the price of it—Rs 30. I shall bring Bari-Bi and Nani to you this evening. The others can stay with me a little longer.'

'Oh, Lala!' said Mother. 'How are we to repay you for all your kindness?'

'I shall be repaid in time to come,' said Lala. 'But what is to become of your dogs?'

'Keep them, Lala, or do what you like with them. It is going to be difficult enough for us to look after ourselves.'

'True,' he said. 'I shall take them with me to Bareilly, and keep them for you.'

He made a low bow to Mother, and left us, and that was the last we saw of him.

We heard later that Lala had taken his family to Bareilly, along with our old servant, Dhani. We never knew what became of the dogs. That evening, Javed Khan had himself gone to Lala's house and brought away Granny and Anet, who were overjoyed to see us. According to the laws of hospitality, food was immediately put before them.

Our party of eight had now been thinned to four. Pilloo and his mother, and Champa, had been left at Lala's house, and we were not to know what became of them until some time afterwards. Javed Khan did not fancy introducing into his household a Firangi boy of fourteen. It was fortunate for Pilloo that he was left behind, otherwise he would surely have been killed by one of the cutthroats who lived in the mohalla near Javed's house.

Pilloo's Fate

In order to preserve some sort of sequence, I must record what happened to the three members of our household who were left at Lala's house.

No sooner had he and Javed Khan left the house with Granny and cousin Anet, that it was beset again by another band of Pathans, headed by one Mangal Khan. He forced his way into the house, the Lala's womenfolk retired to the roof as before, and Pilloo, his mother, and Champa, their servant, shut themselves in their room.

'Where is the Firangi youth?' shouted Mangal Khan. 'Bring him out, so that we may deal with him as we have dealt with others of his kind.'

Seeing that there was no means of escape, Pilloo's mother came out, and falling at Mangal Khan's feet, begged him to spare her son's life.

'*Your* son!' he said, eyeing her disbelivingly from head to foot, for she had a swarthy complexion. 'Let's see what sort of fellow he is.'

Pilloo now came out dressed fantastically, a perfect caricature of a Kayastha boy—pantaloons and shirt; no socks or shoes or headdress—all but his face and fair complexion, which could not be disguised.

'This fellow does not even reach my shoulders,' said Mangal Khan, standing over him. 'How old are you?' he asked sternly.

Pilloo was trembling all over with fright and was unable to answer; instead, he looked at his mother.

She folded her hands and replied, 'Your slave is not more than fourteen, Khan Saheb! I beg of you, spare his life for the Prophet's sake! Do what you like with me, but spare the boy.' And Pilloo's mother rained tears, and fell at his feet again.

The Pathan was moved by these repeated appeals to his feelings.

'Get up, woman!' he said. 'I can see the boy is young and harmless. Will both of you come with me? Remember, if you don't, there are others who will not be as soft-hearted as I.'

Lala's house was obviously no longer safe as a hiding-place, and Pilloo's mother agreed to accompany Mangal Khan. So off they were marched, together with Champa, to another mohalla inhabited chiefly by Pathans, where they were hospitably received at Mangal Khan's house.

Mangal Khan was at heart a generous man. After he had taken the fugitives under his roof, he showed them every kindness and consideration. He called Pilloo by his new name, Ghulam Husain, and his mother continued to be known as Ghulam Husain's mother. Champa, of course, remained Champa. She was a Rajput girl, and there was no mistaking her for anything else.

Pilloo and his mother continued to live under the protection of Mangal Khan. What their subsequent fortunes were we did not know until much later, many months after we had left Lala Ramjimal's house.

Further Alarms

It was in our interests to forget that we had European blood in our veins, and that there was any advantage in the return of the British to power. It was also necessary for us to *seem* to forget that the Christian God was our God, and we allowed it to be believed that we were Muslims. Kothiwali often offered to teach us the *Kalma,* but Mother would reply that she knew it already, which was perfectly true. When she was asked to attend prayers with the others, her excuse would be: 'How can we? Our clothes are unclean and we have no others.'

The only clothes we had were those acquired in Lala Ramjimal's house, and, on our third day in Javed's house, he seemed to notice them for the first time.

'Mariam,' he said. 'It won't do to wear such clothes in my house. You must get into a pyjama.'

'Where have I the means to make pyjamas?' asked Mother.

And the same day Javed went and bought some black chintz in the bazaar, and handed it over to Mother. She made us pyjamas, and kurta-dupattas, cutting the material, while Anet and I did the sewing. Khan-Begum was astonished to find that Mother could cut so well, and that Anet and I were so adept with our needles.

Before we changed into our new clothes, Mother suggested that we be given facilities for bathing. I think we had not bathed for a month, for in Lala's house there was no water close at hand; his womenfolk would bathe every morning at the river, but it had been too dangerous for us to go out.

There was a well right in the middle of the courtyard of Javed Khan's house, and so it was quite possible for us to take a cold bath. Mother told Zeban, the female barber of the house, to draw water for us and help us bathe, and that she would reward this service with a payment of four pice—a pice per person—and Zeban was overjoyed at the prospect of this little windfall. She set up a couple of beds at right angles to one another in the courtyard, covering them with sheets to form a screen. Kothiwali had heard that we were going to change our clothes and bathe, and this being quite an event, she arrived at the house in a great fluster, determined to assist us in the mysteries of the bath.

It was the 2nd of July, a day memorable in our lives from a hygienic point of view.

Kothiwali offered to pour water over us with her own hands. To this, however, Mother strenuously objected. She pointed out that it was not customary among her people to be seen undressed by others, even by members of the same sex, and that she would not therefore, give Kothiwali the trouble.

Kothiwali was dismayed. 'But how can you take the sacred bath and be purified,' she urged, 'unless at least three tumblers of sanctified water are poured on you?'

Mother was ready with her reply. She said that each of us knew the *Kalma,* and that doubtless we would remember the last three tumblers when we came to them. And this embarrasment being overcome, we had the satisfaction of washing our bodies with fresh water from the well, and afterwards, putting on our new clothes, which fitted us perfectly.

After this, we opened our hair to dry, and instantly there were loud exclamations of admiration from the women who were present. Such lovely, long hair! And looking at my curls—my hair was not very long but quite wavy—exclaimed at my pretty *'ghungarwala'*. Mother and Granny did indeed have beautiful heads of hair. Granny's reached down to her heels; Mother's, to a little below the knee. Anet's hair, like mine, reached only to the waist, but it was very bushy, and when made into a plait, was as thick as a fat woman's arm. As we sat about drying our hair, the women gazed at us with their mouths open. We explained that the family from which my mother came was distinguised for the long and bushy hair of its females.

We were also faced with the problem of oiling so much hair, and Khan-Begum asked us what oil we used. Mother said we used coconut oil, but no one knew where so much coconut oil could be had. So Khan-Begum gave a pice to Zeban, and had her fetch us some sweet oil from the bazaar. She also sent for a small fine-tooth comb made of horn. Granny got up and oiled and combed Mother's hair, while Mother dressed mine and Anet's, as well as Granny's.

Next morning we felt buoyant and refreshed. We busied ourselves in sewing a second suit of clothes, which we intended trying on after taking another bath the following Friday, the day of the week on which most Pathan women bathe.

At ten o'clock, Javed Khan received a visitor in the person of Sarfaraz Khan, his wife's brother-in-law. This man had been a constable in the police service, and had retired to his home on the outbreak of the Mutiny. In accordance with the costume of the time, he was armed with sword, pistol, knife and a double-barrelled gun. He appeared excited as he met Javed Khan at the door.

'You have brought some Firangans into the house, Javed?' he said. 'Wouldn't you like to show them to me?'

'You shall see them,' replied Javed, 'and be given the opportunity of appreciating my taste for the beautiful.'

With his hand on his pistol and a menacing look on his bearded face, Sarfaraz Khan strode into the veranda. Khan-Begum stood up and made him a salaam, and we did the same. He sat down on a cot, resting the butt of his gun on the ground, while with one hand he held the barrel—a typical Pathan attitude.

'So these are the Firangans who have made so much stir in the mohalla!' he observed.

Javed Khan had gone into the house, and Mother spoke up for us.

'What stir can we make?' she said. 'We are poor, helpless people.'

'And yet everyone is saying that you have come into this house to find a husband for your daughter, and that Javed Khan is going to marry her! Why have you brought trouble to this good woman?' he said, pointing towards Khan-Begum.

Though Mother was indignant at the insinuation, she restrained her feelings, and answered him quietly.

'What are you saying, brother? Surely you know that we would not have entered this house unless we had been compelled to. Javed Khan brought us here by force, from a house where we had received every kindness, in order to please himself. We are grateful for his hospitality, but as to marrying my daughter to him or to anyone else, that is a matter which I am not in a position to discuss, and we are grateful to your brother for not forcing us to agree to his wishes.'

'And yet it is the talk of the mohalla,' said Sarfaraz Khan, 'that Javed intends marrying your daughter, and this talk has put Khan-Begum in a great state of mind!'

'In what way are we responsible for what people say?' replied Mother. 'We would do anything to save Khan-Begum from unhappiness.'

Javed, who had overheard much of the conversation, now stamped in, looking quite ruffled.

'Brother, what is your motive in questioning this good woman, and treating these people as though they were intruders? By my head, they are in no way to blame! It was I who brought them to my house, and only I am answerable for their actions.'

'Why have you brought trouble to your good wife?' asked

Sarfaraz Khan. 'You have spoilt the good name of our family by your foolish conduct.'

'I know who has sent you here,' remarked Javed, folding his arms across his chest.

'Yes, Abdul Rauf has sent me here to take the women to the riverside, and there strike their heads off, in order that the fire raging in your wife's bosom may be quenched.'

'No one has the right to tell me what I should do in my own house,' said Javed fiercely, drawing himself up to his full height and towering over Sarfaraz Khan. 'If Abdul Rauf is wise, he will look to his own house and family, instead of prying into other people's affairs. I will have none of his interference. As to Qabil, she is a fool for talking too much to the neighbours. I shall have to restrict her liberty.'

The two enraged Pathans would have come to blows, or worse, had not Mother put herself foward again.

'As to cutting off our heads,' she said, 'you have the power, Khan Saheb, and we cannot resist. If it should be Allah's will that we die by your hand, let it be so. There is but one favour, however, that I would ask of you, and that is that you kill every one of us, without exception. I shall not allow you to kill one or two only!'

Sarfaraz Khan was touched, both by Mother's courage, and because she had spoken in the name of Allah. He warmed towards her, as others had done.

'Great is your faith, and great your spirit,' he said. 'Well, I wash my hands off this business. To have been sent on a fool's errand, and to be put off by the calm persuasiveness of a woman!'

'It was Allah's will,' said Javed. 'You will not be so foolish again. Why poison your heart on behalf of your relatives? It was their doing, I knew that all along.'

Another Proposal

Two or three days after the visit of Sarfaraz Khan, when we had taken our evening meal, Javed Khan entered the room and made himself comfortable on the low, wooden platform.

'Mariam, you promised to speak to me again on a certain subject which you know is close to my heart,' he said, addressing Mother. 'Now that you have had time to think it over, perhaps you can give me a definite answer.'

'What subject do you mean?' asked Mother, feigning ignorance.

'I mean my original proposal to marry your daughter.'

'I have hardly had time to argue the matter with myself,' said Mother, 'or to give it the attention it deserves. It was only the other day that your brother-in-law came here to kill us without a moment's notice. If we are likely to be killed even while under your protection, what use is there in discussing the subject of marriage? If I am to lose my life, my daughter's life must go too. She and I are inseparable. Someone like Sarfaraz may be on his way here even now!'

'Upon my head, you make me angry when you talk like that!' exclaimed Javed. 'I tell you that had he lifted his hand against either of you, he would have lost his own life. As long as you are under Javed's roof, there is not a man who would dare to raise his finger against you. I shall strike off the heads of half a dozen, before a hair on my Firangan's head can be touched.' And he gave me a look of such passion and ferocity, that I trembled with fright, and hid my face behind Mother's back.

He was terribly excited, and to calm him, Mother said, 'I am sure you are strong enough to protect us. But why do you bring up this subject again?'

'Because it is always on my mind. Why delay it any longer?'

'If you knew our circumstances and the history of my family,' said Mother, 'you would see that I am not in a position to give her away.'

'Why so?' asked Javed.

'I have my brothers living. What shall I answer them when they find out that I have given you my daughter in marriage, and the girl still only a child? And moreover, my husband's younger brother is still alive. I have to consult them before I can decide anything.'

'That may be so,' said Javed. 'But they are not likely to question you, as in all probability they have been killed along with the other Firangis.'

'I hope not. But would it not be wiser to wait and make certain they are dead before we come to any definite decision?'

'I am an impatient man, Mariam, and life is not so long that I can wait an eternity to quench my desires. I have restrained myself out of respect for your wishes, and out of respect for you. But my desire to call your girl my wife grows stronger daily, and I am prepared to take any risk to have her for my own.'

'Suppose the English Government is restored to power—what shall we do then? Your life will be worth little, and with you dead, my daughter will be a widow at thirteen. Cannot you wait a few months, until we are certain as to who will remain masters of this country?'

'True, if the English retook Shahjahanpur, they would show little mercy to the leaders of the revolt. They would hang me from the nearest tree. And no doubt you are hoping for their return, or you would not talk of such a possibility. But how many of them are left? Only a few thousand struggling to hold their own before the walls of Delhi, and they too will soon be disposed of, please God!'

'Then let Delhi decide our future,' said Mother, seizing at a straw. 'If the British army now besieging Delhi is destroyed, that will be the time to talk of such matters. Meanwhile, are we not your dependents and in your power? You have only to await the outcome of the war.'

'You point a long way off, Mariam, and seem to forget that I have the power to marry her against your will and the will of everyone else, including'—and he gave his wife a defiant look—'the owner of a pair of jealous eyes now gazing at me!'

'Did I say you did not have that power?' asked Mother. 'If you take her by force, we have no power to resist. But it would be unmanly of you to compel a fatherless child to gratify your desires. What merit would there be in that? Whereas, if you were to wait until the British are driven from Delhi, my argument would no longer carry any weight. And by that time, my daughter would be more of an age for marriage.'

'It is fortunate for you that I am a man. No one shall take her away from Javed, and Javed's wife she shall be, and I will give her a handsome dowry. And if you were to take my advice, Mariam, you ought to take a husband as well, and settle down again in life. You are still young.'

'Why would I marry now?'

'You should marry, if it be only to find a home of your own, and bread, with it.'

'Why would I marry?' asked Mother again. 'What would become of my girls?'

'Why, your daughter shall be mine,' said Javed brightly. 'And as to your niece, she too will fit in somewhere! She is not unattractive, you know!'

We did not speak much for the rest of the evening. Javed Khan settled himself before a hookah, puffing contentedly, blissfully unaware of the agitation he had set up in everyone's minds. No one spoke. Khan-Begum went about with a long face, and sighed whenever she looked at me. Mother, too, sighed when she looked at me, and Anet and I stared at each other in bewilderment.

As we rose to go to our part of the house, Khan-Begum seized Mother's hand, and in a choking voice, whispered, 'Mariam, you are my mother. Do not help him to inflict greater torment on me than I have already suffered. Promise me that you won't give your daughter to him.'

Mother replied, 'Bibi, you have seen and heard everything that has happened. I am truly a dead one in the hands of the living. You distress yourself for nothing. If I have my way, he shall never get my consent. But will he wait for my consent?'

'Allah bless you!' exclaimed Khan-Begum. 'Your daughter deserves a better fate than to play second fiddle in this family. I will pray that your wishes are granted.'

I could not sleep much that night. The light from the full moon came through the high, barred window, and fell across the foot of the bed. I dozed a little, but the insistent call of the brain-fever bird kept waking me. I opened my eyes once, and saw Javed Khan standing in the doorway, the moonlight shining on his face. He stood there a long while, staring at me, and I was too afraid to move or call out. Then he turned and walked quietly away; and shivering with fright, I put my arms around Mother, and lay clinging to her for the remainder of the night.

On Show

When Khan-Begum had last visited her husband's sister, the latter had made her promise to come again soon; and on a Thursday, a servant came to her with a message, saying, 'Your sister sends her salaams, and wishes to know when you are going to fulfil your promise of calling on her?'

'Give my respects to my sister,' answered Khan-Begum, 'and tell her I cannot come now. There are some Firangans staying with us, brought into the house by my husband.'

Later, another messenger arrived with the suggestion that Khan-Begum take her guests along with her, as her relatives were most anxious to see them too. And so our hostess proposed that we accompany her to her sister Qamran's house the next morning.

Four of us set out in one *meana*: Khan-Begum, Mother, Anet and myself. Granny was left behind.

A *meana* is something like a palanquin of old, but smaller, and used exclusively for the conveyance of women. It has short, stubby legs to rest on the ground, the floor is interlaced with string, and the top is covered with red curtains, hanging down the sides. The bearers fix two bamboo poles on either side, by which they lift the *meana* from the ground.

Supported by four perspiring bearers, we arrived at Qamran's house, where we were kindly received. Qamran had at first been prejudiced against us, but the report taken to her by Sarfaraz Khan, had made her change her views. She was eager to make our acquaintance, and pressed us to stay with her; and during the weeks to come, we were to be her showpieces, on display for those who wanted to see us.

Sarfaraz Khan had come to Javed's house with the intention of striking off our heads, but Mother's charm had baffled him and won him over. Returning home, he had said, 'Who can lift his hand against such harmless things? The girl is like a frightened doe, and the mother, she is a perfect nightingale!' And so, among those who came to see us at Qamran's house was Sarfaraz Khan's wife, Hashmat. She, too, fell a victim to mother's charm. 'Oh sister!' she exclaimed to Khan-Begum. 'My husband was quite right in his opinion of them. Mariam's lips, like the bee, distil nothing but honey.'

As to Qamran herself, her soft, sympathetic nature was roused by the story of our bereavement and our trials. Her large, pretty, black eyes would fill with tears as she listened to Mother, and once she placed her head on Mother's shoulder and sobbed aloud.

She was about thirty-five, and on the verge of becoming stout; but she had fine features and a clear complexion. We were told that when she was dressed for her marriage, her father passed by, and was so struck by her beauty, that he exclaimed: 'Couldn't we have reserved so much beauty for someone who did not have to go out of our family!'

Qamran's husband, a much older man, was a cavalry lieutenant in the army at Bhopal. At their first meeting, she had felt a repugnance for his person. She repelled his advances, and would not allow him even to touch her, with the result that her mother and others began to believe that she was in love with a jinn, or spirit. It suited her to encourage them in this belief. Her husband was disgusted, and returned to his cavalry regiment, but continued to keep her supplied with funds. Eventually, through the good offices of mutual friends, they were reconciled, and were blessed with a daughter, whom they named Badran.

Badran's beauty was different from her mother's. At the time we saw her she was sixteen or seventeen; she was slightly darker than her mother, and her eyes, though large, lacked the liquid softness which gave such serenity to Qamran's face. But a pink birthmark on her left cheek gave her an interesting face. She did not have her mother's liveliness or enquiring nature, and we did not see much of her.

Qamran had heard of our skill with the needle. She had made up her mind to make a present to her sister-in-law's small son, and asked us if we would help make the kurta-topi, which would consist of miniature trousers, coat and cap. Mother offered to cut and sew them.

She gave the kurta, which was of purple cloth, a moghlai neck; that is, it had one opening, buttoning to the side over the left shoulder. It was finished off with gold lace round the edges and sleeves and neck. She also gave it a crescent-shaped, gold-embroidered band round the neck, and epaulettes on the shoulders. The trousers were made of rich, green satin, and also finished off with gold lace. The cap was made of the same stuff as the coat, and had several gold pendants tacked round in front, so that it formed a kind of fillet, resting on the forehead. The three garments cost Qamran something like forty rupees—a sumptuous suit for a child!

Mother was pleased with the result of her work, and all who saw the suit were in raptures, and Qamran made Mother a present of a new set of bangles, made of glass and enamelled blue.

We soon established ourselves as favourites in Qamran's house, and members of the household vied with each other in showing us kindness. Whereas they had formerly believed that, as Firangi women, we would be peeping out of doors and windows in order to be seen by men, without whose society European women were supposed to be unable to live, they were agreeably surprised to find that we delighted in hard work, that we loved needles and thread, and that, far from seeking the company of men, we did our best to avoid them.

'You are like one of us,' said Qamran to Mother one day. 'I would not exchange you for half-a-dozen women of my own race. Who could possibly ever tire of you?'

Politics seldom ever entered the four walls of the zenana—wars and deeds of violence were considered the prerogative of men. Seldom was any reference made to the disturbances that were taking place throughout the country, or to our own troubles. Only once was the even tenor of our lives disturbed, and that was due to the woman, Umda, who had taken a jealous dislike to us from the beginning.

I do not know in what way she was related to Qamran, but they addressed each other as 'sister', and Badran called her 'aunt'. She was a spiteful young woman, with a sharp, lashing tongue, very hostile towards all foreign races. She had been very displeased at our introduction into the family, always gave us angry looks, and never missed an opportunity to speak ill of us.

It pleased Umda to hear of the British reverses, and she was convinced that they would be swept from the walls of Delhi. Occasionally, she would leave aside generalities, and give her attention to individuals.

Once Mother, Anet and I sat quietly together, sewing a pair of pyjamas for Badran, while Badran herself, sat at the end of the veranda, whispering nonsense to her good-natured young husband, Hafizulla Khan. He, however, had his eyes on Umda, for he knew her well.

She began by changing the conversation with a contemptuous reference to the Firangi race, bringing up the old story of the hunger of European women for male company.

'Those wantons!' she said. 'They cannot live without the society of men.'

'Perhaps not, *chachi*,' observed Hafizulla Khan from the other end of the veranda, 'and perhaps they are quite right in doing so. They have so much of male company that their appetite for it is probably less than yours. And then not all their men are opium-eaters like your husband, who, beyond rolling in the dust like a pig, has little time for anything else.'

'That may be so,' she said haughtily, 'but what has it to do with Firangi women? You cannot deny that they enjoy laughing and joking with strange men, that they dance and sing, sometimes half-nude, and with the arms of strange men round their waists. Then they retire into dark corners where they kiss and are kissed by others than their husbands!'

Badran's bright eyes had grown wide with astonishment at this recital of the ways of the Firangi female.

'I did not know all that,' said Hafizulla Khan. 'From where do you obtain your deep knowledge, *chachi*?'

'Never mind where,' she replied impatiently. 'It is true what I have said, and that's why I say these Firangans will prove troublesome.'

'Now you are going too far, *chachi*,' said Hafizulla. 'Upon my head, you are very careless in what you say. What charge can you bring against our guests here?'

'Well, when they first entered Javed's house, there was some excitement among the men in the neighbourhood.'

'Quite possibly,' said Hafizulla with sarcasm. 'Your good husband was a little excited too, I suppose. Well, what came of it?'

'You are a funny boy, Hafiz!' she said mischievously, giving him a knowing wink in full sight of us. 'What are your intentions, eh?'

'You are behaving very stupidly today, *chachi*!' said Hafizulla, growing impatient. 'What do you insinuate by that shake of your unbalanced head? I tell you again, be careful how you speak of Mariam and her daughter!'

'The boy stands as a champion of the white brood! Well, I have no patience with them.'

There was a pause in the contention. Mother, Anet and I had remained absolutely silent during this heated conversation; we were not in a position to say anything in our own defence, for we were in Qamran's house only on sufferance, and had no right to quarrel with anyone; and at the same time, we could not have improved on Hafizulla's performance.

Umda was bent on mischief and would not change the subject. 'My son has gone with the expedition. I hope and pray that he does not bring a Firangi female back with him.'

Hafizulla was ready for her. 'No doubt your son will perform deeds of great valour on his expedition, but considering that it is only a few refractory landowners that they have been sent to quell, I don't think there is any chance of his finding any Firangans to come back with.'

Before Umda could take up the cudgels again, Hafizulla got to his feet and told her that it was time she returned to her own house; that he did not intend sitting by to hear us abused by her. But Umda was determined to have the last word.

'Great is the power of prayer,' she said. 'I have advised Khan-Begum to take ashes in her hand, and blow them towards these women, that they might fly away like this.' And throwing a pinch of dust towards us, she mumbled something under her breath.

It was too much for Hafizulla Khan. He rushed at Umda and dragged her out of the veranda. Then telling her to be gone, or he would be more rough with her, he returned and sat down near his wife, in a great rage.

The Rains

'It does not surprise me,' said Qamran, when she came home and heard of the quarrel between Umda and her son-in-law. 'Umda has too long and too venomous a tongue altogether. What business is it of hers that you should be my guests? She might have taken a lesson from you in patience and forbearance. Son!' she said, addressing Hafizulla. 'You need not have dragged her out. Nevertheless, it was noble of you to have taken the side of these unfortunate ones. Mariam, forgive her for her foolishness. She has only succeeded in giving the young an opportunity to jeer at her. In my house you will always be welcome.'

It was now the height of the rainy season, and heavy clouds were banking in the west. A breeze brought us the fresh scent of approaching rain, and presently we heard the patter of raindrops on the jasmine bushes that grew in the courtyard.

It was the day of the festival observed throughout northern India by the womenfolk, who put on their most colourful costumes, and relax on innumerable swings, giving release to feelings of joy and abandon. Double ropes are suspended from a tree, and the ends are knotted together and made to hold narrow boards painted in gay colours. Two women stand facing each other, having taken each other's ropes by catching them between their toes. They begin to swing gently, gradually moving faster and higher, until they are just a brightly coloured blur against the green trees and grey skies. Sometimes, a small bed is fixed between the ropes, on which two or three can sit, while two others move the swing, singing to them at the same time.

A swing having been put up from an old banyan tree that grew just behind the house, Badran and Hashmat, both dressed in red from head to foot, climbed on to it. Anet and I swung them, while Gulabia, the servant-girl, sang. When they came down we had our turn, and I found it an exhilarating experience, riding through the air, watching the racing clouds above me at one moment, and Anet's dark curls below me at the next. Removed for a while from the world below, I felt again that life could be gay and wonderful.

Mother's memory was stored with an incredible amount of folklore, and she would sometimes astonish our hosts with her references to sprites and evil spirits. One day Badran, having taken her bath, came out into the courtyard with her long hair lying open.

'My girl, you ought not to leave your hair open,' said Mother. 'It is better to make a knot in it.'

'But I have not yet oiled it,' said Badran. 'How can I put it up?'

'It is not wise to leave it open when you sit outside in the cool of the evening.'

'Do tell me why,' said Badran. 'See, I will do as you say and give it a knot for the present.' And she pressed Mother to tell her why it was unsafe to leave her hair open in the evening.

'There are aerial beings called jinns, who are easily attracted by long hair and pretty black eyes like yours,' said Mother.

Badran blushed, her mother and husband both being present; and Qamran smiled at the recollection of her own youthful waywardness, when she made everyone believe that she was the object of a jinn's passion.

'Do the jinns visit human beings?' asked Hafizulla Khan.

'So it is said,' said Mother. 'I have never seen a jinn myself, but I have noticed the effect they have on others.'

'Oh, please tell us what you have seen,' begged Qamran.

'There was once a lovely girl who had a wealth of black hair,' said Mother. 'Quite unexpectedly she became seriously ill, and inspite of every attention and the best medical advice, she grew worse every day. She became as thin as a whipping-post, and lost all her beauty, with the exception of her hair, which remained beautiful and glossy until her dying day. Whenever she fell asleep, she would be tormented by dreams. A young jinn would appear to her, and tell her that he had fallen in love with her beautiful hair one evening as she was drying it after a bath, and that he intended to take her away. She was in great pain, yet in the midst of her sufferings, her invisible tormentor never ceased to visit her; and though her body became shrivelled, there shone in her eyes an unearthly light; and when her body decayed and died, her gorgeous head of hair remained as beautiful as ever.'

'What a dreadful story!' said Badran, hurriedly tying another knot in her hair.

Conversation then turned upon different types of ghosts and spirits, and Qamran told us about the *Munjia*—the disembodied spirit of a Brahmin youth who has died before his marriage—which is supposed to have its abode in a peepul tree. When the *Munjia* gets annoyed, it rushes out from the tree and upsets bullock-carts, *meanas* and even horse-driven carriages. Should anyone be passing beneath a lonely peepul tree at night, advised Qamran, one should not make the mistake of yawning without snapping one's fingers in front of one's mouth.

'If you don't remember to do this,' said Qamran, 'the *Munjia* will dash down your throat and completely ruin you.'

Mother then launched into an account of the various types of ghosts she was acquainted with: the ghosts of immoral women—*churels*—who appear naked, with their feet facing backwards; ghosts with long front teeth, which suck human blood; and ghosts which take the form of animals. In some of the villages near Rampur (according to Mother), people have a means by which they can tell what form a departed person has taken in the next life. The ashes are placed in a basin and left outside at night, covered with a heavy lid. Next morning, a footprint can be seen in the ashes. It may be the footprint of a man or a bird or an elephant, according to the form taken by the departed spirit.

By ten o'clock we were feeling most reluctant to leave each other's company on the veranda. It did not make us feel any better to be told by mother and Qamran to recite certain magical verses to keep away evil spirits. When I got into bed I couldn't lie still, but kept twisting and turning and looking at the walls for moving shadows. After some time, we heard a knocking on our door, and the voices of Badran and Hashmat. Getting up and opening it, we found them looking pale and anxious. Qamran had succeeded in frightening them, too.

'Are you all right, Khurshid?' they asked. 'Wouldn't you like to sleep in our room? It might be safer. Come, we'll help you to carry your bed across.'

'We are quite all right here,' protested Mother, but we were hustled along to the next room, as though a band of ghosts was conspiring against us. Khan-Begum had been absent during all this activity (though she had been present during the story-telling), and the first we heard of her was a loud cry. We ran towards the sound and found her emerging from our room.

'Mariam has disappeared!' she cried. 'Khurshid and Anet have gone too!'

And then, when she saw us come running out of her own room, our hair loose and disordered, she gave another cry and fainted on the veranda.

White Pigeons

'You are bearing your troubles very well,' said Hafizulla to mother one evening. 'You are so cheerful and patient, and you seem to look forward to the future with hope. And after all, what is the good of mourning for a past which can never return again?'

'I doubt if there can be any improvement in their situation,' said Khan-Begum. 'Only yesterday the fakir was saying that the Firangis had been wiped off the face of the land.'

'I am not so sure of that,' remarked Hafizulla.

'Nor I,' said Qamran. 'The fact is, we do not get much news here.'

'Well, I can tell you something,' said Hafizulla. 'Though my uncle did boast the other day that there were no Firangis left, I overheard him whispering to Sarfaraz Khan that they were not yet totally extinct. The hills are full of them. My uncle was relating how Abdul Rauf Khan had gone on the morning of Id to pay his respects to Mian Saheb, the same fakir you speak of, and he was astounded by what the old man told him.'

'What was it?' urged Khan-Begum.

'Abdul Rauf said that Mian Saheb was in a strange mood. He cast off the white clothes which he had been wearing during the past three months and, very suddenly, and without apparent reason, put on a black robe. Abdul Rauf and the others had gone to him to ask that he pray for the defeat of the Firangis before Delhi, but what do you think he told them?'

Hafizulla paused dramatically, and both Qamran and Khan-Begum said at the same time, 'What did he tell them?'

'He told them that the restoration of the Firangi rule was as certain as the coming of doomsday. It would be another hundred years, he said, before the foreigners could be made to leave. "See, here they come!" he cried, pointing to the north where a flock of white pigeons could be seen hovering over the city. "They come flying like white pigeons which, when disturbed, fly away, and circle, and come down to rest again. White pigeons from the hills!" Abdul Rauf folded his hands and begged Mian Saheb to say no more. But the Mian is no respecter of persons, and his words are not to be taken lightly.'

Our stay with Qamran was drawing to a close. We had passed almost the entire rainy season in the company of her agreeable household, and time had passed swiftly. We could not have received greater kindness or sympathy than we had been given by Qamran, and her son-in-law, Hafizulla. Javed Khan had been several times to see us— or rather, to see his wife and sister. Once or twice he had pressed Qamran to shorten our stay, but she did not want us to leave, and kept us on the pretext that we were sewing some things for her, which were not quite ready. He did not press her too much, as he knew that having both his wife and us under his roof did not make things easier for him.

Though appointed by the Nawab to a military command, we did not hear that Javed had engaged in any new or daring enterprise. His sacking of the Rosa Rum Factory had been his chief exploit to date, and that too, had been done more for personal gain than from any other motive. He had shown no enthusiasm for the massacre at Muhamdi, where a company of sepoys had finished off the few Europeans who had managed to get away from Shahjahanpur. Now he limited his services to attending the Nawab's receptions, and to keeping him informed of news from Delhi and the whereabouts of stray refugees and survivors like ourselves. We heard, for instance, of the hiding-place of the Redmans. A beggar woman happened to be passing before the house of the Redmans' old washerwoman, and stopping there to beg, recognized the tall, fair woman sitting in the yard.

'Who are you, eh?' she cackled. 'I know who you are! And where are your white husband and son?'

'Be off, *churel*!' said Mrs Redman. 'Go about your begging, and do not interfere with my affairs.'

Meanwhile the dhobi came home and, taking in the situation, told the beggar woman, 'How do you know she is a Firangan? She happens to be my sister-in-law.'

'Very fair for one of your caste!' said the old woman slyly.

'Ask any more questions, and my washing-board will descend on your head!' threatened the dhobi. 'Be off, dead one!'

The beggar woman hobbled off, cursing both the dhobi's family and the Redmans, and made her way to Abdul Rauf Khan's house, where she informed him of what she had discovered. Abdul Rauf took his information to the Nawab, and suggested that he be permitted to capture the Firangan.

'That would be an adventure worthy of you,' said the amused Nawab. 'No doubt you would need an armed detachment to capture her. But I prefer not to hound these refugees, Khan Saheb. They have not done our cause any harm.' And he showed them the same forbearance that he had shown us.

The season of Moharram, had come and gone. We did not even notice that it was over, for there were very few Shia families in Shahjahanpur, and the festival was not kept up with the same zeal that was shown in other towns. Unlike the Shia women, the Pathan women do not go into mourning during the ten days of fasting, nor do they remove their ornaments. Food and clothing were, however, sent to the nearest mosque to be distributed among the poor of the city.

Moharram over, it was decided that we should return to Javed Khan's house on Friday, the 4th of September.

The Impatience of Javed Khan

Poor Khan-Begum was to suffer many more pangs of jealousy before she could be done with us. On the same day that we returned to her house, Javed Khan took the opportunity to question Mother again, regarding her plans for my marriage.

'Tell me, Mariam, how much longer am I to wait?' he asked after dinner.

'What can I say?' sighed Mother. 'You ask me so often. I have already told you that I cannot give my daughter away without consulting my brothers. You had agreed to wait until the contest before Delhi was decided.'

'May the Firangi name perish, I say!' he exclaimed furiously. 'Surely your brothers have all been exterminated by now!' Then, his mood changing suddenly from anger to a brooding sullenness, he muttered to himself: 'Perhaps the fellow spoke the truth when he said, "Subedarji, will you reach Delhi at all?" For Ghansham Singh was not fated to set foot within the walls of the city. He fell at the Hindan bridge, when the Firangi army attacked the Bareilly brigade. He could not tell the King of our achievements here on the 31st of May. Well, I have done my part—and the sugar loaf solved my sherbet problem at Moharram. I would also have dealt well with that boy at Mangal Khan's, but the fool, Mangal, came between us and said he had adopted the boy as his own son. I never heard of a true believer adopting an infidel—a plague on them all!'

His face was dark and threatening as he went out of the house, and after a few minutes, we were startled by the screams of the boy Saifulla, Javed's half-brother, who had bumped into Javed in the lane and upon whom the Pathan was now venting his rage and frustration.

Javed Khan had stripped the boy to the waist, and taking out his horsewhip, had lashed the boy so severely, that the skin was actually torn from his back. Saifulla was laid up for several days, yelling from the pain which the festered parts gave him; but instead of softening towards him, Javed Khan threatened to repeat the flogging if the boy didn't stop groaning.

I have no doubt that it was Mother's disappointing answer that had driven Javed into a frenzy, and I suppose I should have been grateful that his passion had found an outlet on the back of his brother. Javed hated the boy for being the offspring of an illicit affair of his father's.

That same evening, Javed gave a further display of his savage disposition. Having enquired from the syce whether his horse had received its gram, and having been informed that Rupia, the servant-woman, had not yet ground it, he called the woman and demanded to know why the gram had not yet been ground.

'I was busy with other things,' she explained.

'Were you, you dead one?' he shouted fiercely, and seizing his whip again, laid it on her so violently, that she was literally made black and blue, and her torn and scanty clothes were cut to rags. She was bedridden for several days. Every one in the house went about in apprehension, wondering what Javed's next outburst would be like, but Mother could not bear to hear the groans of the woman and the boy. She had Zeban fetch some ground turmeric, which she heated on the fire and applied to the bruises. She attended to them for three days until their wounds began to heal.

One day Javed approached Mother again, and we were afraid there would be a repetition of his earlier display of temper; but he looked crestfallen, and was probably a little ashamed of his behaviour. He complained of having pains all over his body, and begged Mother to tell him of a remedy.

'You have been prescribing for those two wretches,' he said. 'Can't you give me something too?'

'What can I give you?' replied mother. 'I am not a hakim. When I was in my senses I might have been able to think of something for your pain. You look very well, I must say.'

'I am not well,' said Javed. 'I cannot sit on my horse as well as usual. It is all due to my disregard for the wisdom of my betters: "Don't shoot on a Thursday." Last Thursday when I went out shooting, I saw a black buck and fired at it, but I missed, and instead, I hit a white pigeon sitting on a tomb. The pigeon flew into a bush, and I could not find it; but it must have been killed. I got nothing that day, and when I returned home in the evening, I felt exhausted and quite unable to use my limbs. I was as stiff as a dead one. Abdul Rauf was informed, and when he heard of what had happened he came to see me, very angry, because I had fired on the bird. "Pigeons," he said, "are people who come out of their graves on Thursdays for a little fresh air." Well, Abdul Rauf had me treated, shut me in a room, and eventually I came to myself. But I have this swelling on my face, where the dead one must have slapped me.'

His face did appear to be slightly swollen; but, before Mother could take a closer look, Javed started at the sound of music in the street. His face underwent a violent change and, taking down his whip, he rushed out of the house.

There was a great deal of commotion outside, and then we heard the sound of someone shouting: *'Hai! Hai!* Save me, I am being murdered!'

We all looked at each other in wonder, and Khan-Begum said, 'It must be that boy who passes this way sometimes, singing and playing love songs on his flute. My husband swore, by the soul of his dead father, to flog the fellow within an inch of his life if he caught him singing before this house.'

'But what harm is done by his singing?' asked Mother.

'None that I know of. But in a Pathan settlement, no one is allowed to sing or play any instrument in the streets. Music is supposed to excite all sorts of passions, and so it is discouraged.'

'Still, I do not see what right our protector has to assault another in the street merely because he is singing and playing his flute. Is Javed not afraid that he might have to answer to the Nawab for his high-handedness?'

Khan-Begum began to laugh. 'The Nawab?' she said. 'Of what are you thinking, Mariam? Why should the Nawab care about it?'

A Visit from Kothiwali

It was the 13th of September, a Sunday morning, when the family barber, brought a message from Kothiwali to Javed Khan. 'Your *chachi* sends you her salaams, and says she intends to pay you a visit tomorrow.' To this Javed Khan sent the reply: 'It is my *chachi's* house, let her come and throw the light of her presence on it.' Messages of this sort were always couched in extremely polite language.

The following morning Kothiwali arrived in her *meana*, attended by her servants. We were glad to see her again, as she was always so friendly.

'Now, Mariam, I have come to ask you to spend some time with me. I am seething with jealousy because you spent so much time at Qamran's house. Javed, you have no objection to my taking them with me?'

'It is all the same to me whether they stay here or go with you,' said Javed Khan with a shrug of his shoulders.

'Why so?' asked Kothiwali mischievously. 'I thought you were unhappy unless they were under your own roof ?'

'True, but what good is it?' he said. 'My ambition was to possess the girl.'

'Well, she is in your possession now, isn't she?' said Kothiwali.

'Upon my head, you are exasperating!' exclaimed Javed. 'So far as her presence in my house goes, she is in my possession, but what of that? I would marry her today, if it were not for her mother's procrastinations! Sometimes it is: "I have not consulted my brothers," as if she had any brothers left to consult. Sometimes it is: "Wait until the fighting before Dilli is over," as if, even when it is over, it will make any great difference to people like us. It is foolish to expect that the Firangis will be victorious. Have I not seen a score of them running for their lives pursued by one of our soldiers?'

'Perhaps, but it is not always like that,' said Kothiwali.

'I wonder why your sympathies are with them, *chachi* ?'

'Well, they have always been quite good to me,' she replied. 'When my husband was killed by his enemies, it was the Collector who came to my house to condole with me, and it was he who saw to it that our fields were not taken from us. True, that was a long time ago. But I have no reason to wish them ill. At the same time, don't think I wish to run down the cause you have made your own—the rebel cause, I mean.'

'The *rebel* cause! Why do you always call it the rebel cause, *chachi* ?' Javed Khan looked very upset. 'Rebels against whom? Against aliens! Are they not to be expelled from the land? To fight them is not rebellion, but a meritorious act, surely!'

'Maybe, if it doesn't involve the murder of innocent women and children. But see how the Firangis are holding out before Delhi!'

'Enough, *chachi*. Say no more, or you will rouse the demon in me. Let us not anticipate events. Delhi still stands, and Bahadur Shah reigns!'

'Nevertheless, I would advise you to take Mariam's suggestion and wait until the siege is raised. Be cautious, Javed, in your designs on this girl.'

'I have need to be, no doubt, after hearing about the example set by the Kanpur girl.'

'Oh! And who was she?'

'The General's daughter. A girl still beautiful at the age of twenty. She was saved from the massacre by Jamadar Narsingh, one of Nana Saheb's bodyguards, who would have liked to make her his wife. His intentions, like mine, were probably quite honourable, but Zerandaz Khan, another officer, stole the girl one night from the Jamadar's house, and treated her so savagely, that he roused in her all the pride and resentment of her race. For some time she concealed her feelings, but one night, when he was asleep, she drew his scimitar from under his pillow and plunged it into his breast. She then went and threw herself in a well. That was pluck and daring wasn't it, *chachi*? But,'—pointing at me, though looking away,—'I have not even looked her full in the face, believe me!'

'Ah, you sly man!' said Kothiwali jestingly.

There was a pause, at the end of which, Kothiwali said, 'They may come with me, Javed, can't they? You are in a surly mood this morning.'

'Oh yes, take them with you,' he muttered sulkily. 'If they are happier with you, they may go with you.'

Seated in the same *meana* as Kothiwali, we were carried along to her house. I should really call it a mansion, because it was a large, brick building with a high entrance and a spacious courtyard. There was also a set of glass-roofed chambers over the gateway, which the men used as retiring rooms; while the women's apartments were situated on the ground floor, and were cool and spacious.

The family consisted of Kothiwali, her daugher and two sons, one daugher-in-law, one son-in-law, and innumerable grandchildren. Kothiwali was the widow of a landed proprietor in the District, and must have been about forty years old when we knew her. She was tall, with black hair and eyes, a large mouth, small teeth, coloured black with *missi* and paan. She wore no trinkets except for a round silver bangle on each hand, and a plain silver ring on her right small finger. Her face was always cheerful, and she possessed great spirit. She commanded great respect from the rest of her community, who often came to consult her when in difficulty.

Mother soon became a favourite in the household, and so did Anet and I, but to a lesser degree. Kothiwali paid special attention to us. 'What quiet girls they are!' she would sometimes say. 'They never waste their time in idle talk.'

'Why not have the girls' ears and noses bored?' she said to Mother one day.

'What would be the good when I have nothing to make them wear,' replied mother.

The lobes of our ears were already bored, and I was glad I did not have to submit to having my nose bored as well.

'I am glad you did not submit to Javed's request for your daughter's hand in marriage,' said Kothiwali. 'Had she been my daughter, I would never have agreed. Javed is very inconstant.'

'It would have been an incongruous match,' said Mother. 'My poor husband could never have imagined that she would be sought for by a Pathan as his second wife!'

Kothiwali's elder son, Wajihulla Khan, came in and sat down while we were talking. He was a young man of twenty-five, a hafiz—one who knows the *Quran* by heart—and regular at his prayers: it was he who gave the call to prayer in the neighbouring mosque. He was fair, of medium height, and quiet and respectful in his manner. His usual haunt was the bungalow over the gateway, where he spent most of his time reading or playing chess—a game which is now losing much of its popularity. He came in with a friend named Kaddu Khan, a very handsome young man, who called Kothiwali, *chachi*. I think I recognized him as one of the band who had forced us to leave Lala Ramjimal's house. He was suffering from consumption in its first stage, and Wajihulla joined Kothiwali in begging Mother to prescribe something for him.

'I am not a doctor,' said Mother. 'I know the remedies for some minor ailments, but I very much doubt if I could help this boy.'

'No, do not refuse to do something for him,' urged Wajihulla. 'He is really a man of an adventurous spirit, though he has yet to gain fame for his achievements.'

'Do not make fun of the poor fellow,' said Kothiwali. 'He looks sufficiently depressed already.'

'No, I shall relate his worthy deeds to *mausi,* before I ask her to give him something to improve his condition.'

Kaddu Khan now looked more dejected than ever and hung his handsome head in acute embarrassment.

'To begin with, *mausi,* this is the gentleman who proposed to Nawab Qadar Ali to dig up the Christian graves for the treasure which, he was sure, was buried there.'

Kaddu Khan looked up and said, 'So I was made to believe. And the fox who gave me that information, also told me that when a Firangi dies, two bags of money are buried with him.'

'And of course, you believed that absurd story, and went about digging up their bones? Tell us what treasure you found!'

'We began digging at night,' said Kaddu Khan, deciding it would be better if he told the story himself. 'It was a moonlit night. There were three of us. I volunteered to go down into the grave and bring up anything valuable that I could find. To keep in touch with my comrades, we hammered a peg in the ground above and fastened a rope to it, and with its help, I slipped down. But imagine my horror when, instead of touching firm ground, I found myself hanging between heaven and earth! I let out a cry of distress. My comrades, instead of helping me out, thought the Firangi devils were after us, and instantly took to their heels, leaving me dangling over the grave.'

'A situation you had merited,' observed Wajihulla. 'But tell us how you got out.'

'I hung on to the rope and with a great deal of effort managed to raise myself to the bank. And now I tried to follow the example of my brave companions by making a run for it, but as I got up to do so, I felt a violent jerk around my waist and fell down again. Again I tried to get up and run, and again I was pulled to the ground. I was half-dead through fright, but I made one last lunge forward, and this time the wooden peg came up too, and I lost no time in taking to my heels. *Chachi,* that graveyard is full of Firangi devils!'

'What a thick-headed fellow you are!' said Wajihulla, enjoying himself immensely. 'One would think there could be some sense beneath that beautiful brow of yours. It was your waistband, Kaddu, that got hammered down with the peg. It left you dangling over the grave, and when you tried to run, it pulled you down again. It was only when you pulled the peg up that your cummerbund was loosened.'

Kothiwali and the rest of us had a good laugh at Kaddu Khan's discomfiture.

'It should serve as a lesson to you,' said Kothiwali, 'that all men are alike when the time comes to die. When you are dead would you like somebody to disturb your body in search of treasure? Treasure indeed! Even kings go empty-handed when they die. A child, when it is born, comes into the world with a closed fist, and the same hand lies open and flat at the time of death. We bring nothing into the world, and we take nothing out!'

At this juncture, Kaddu Khan's mother and sister joined us and, folding their hands to Mother, entreated her to do something for the youth.

They had conceived an exaggerated idea of Mother's powers of healing. All she told Kaddu to do was to take a dose of *khaksir* tea every six hours, and to abstain from acidic and hot food; and she told him to chew some fresh coconut every morning, drinking the juice as well. Kaddu Khan tried these simple remedies, and we heard that he eventually got better.

The Fall of Delhi

We were sitting in the veranda with Kothiwali when there was a disturbance in the next porch, where most of the men were sitting. Javed Khan had just ridden up, and had whispered something in Sarfaraz Khan's ear. Sarfaraz got up immediately and came and whispered something to Kothiwali. As soon as he had gone, Kothiwali turned to Mother and said, 'Well, Mariam, Delhi has been taken by the Firangis. What great changes will take place now . . . .'

Our hearts leapt at the news, and tears came to our eyes, for a British victory meant a release from our confinement and state of dependence; but Delhi was a far cry from Shahjahanpur, and we did not give any expression to our feelings.

On the contrary, Mother took Kothiwali's hand and said, 'May you have peace out of it, too, Pathani.'

'Javed Khan will look quite small now, won't he?' said Kothiwali merrily. Apparently the news did not affect her one way or the other: she dealt in individuals, not in communities. 'But he has good reason to be worried. The Firangis will have heavy scores to settle in this city.'

The next day the menfolk held a long discussion. Some spoke of fleeing the city, others suggested that it would be better to wait and watch the course of events.

Sarfaraz Khan: 'Though Delhi has fallen to the Firangi army, it will be a long time before a small town like ours can be reoccupied. Our soldiers, who have been driven from Delhi, will make a stand at some other important place, Lucknow perhaps, and it will be months before we see a Firangi uniform in Shahjahanpur. Do not be in a hurry to run away, unless, of course, you have special reasons to be afraid of an avenging army . . . .'

Javed: 'True, very true, *bhai*. I have done nothing to be afraid of. Have I, now? It's fellows like Abdul Rauf, who served under the Firangis and then threw in their lot with the sepoys, that are sure to be hung. As for me, I never did take salt with the Firangis. If it comes to the worst, I shall ride across the border into Nepal, or take service in the Gwalior brigade.'

Sarfaraz: 'Oh, I'm sure you will. But why leave the city at all if there is nothing to be afraid of?'

Hafizulla: 'I saw some of our men who had returned from Delhi. They were lucky to get away. They had on only their tattered tunics and shorts.'

'Did they say anything of the fighting at Delhi?' asked Sarfaraz Khan.

'They told me that our army was not able to make much impression on the *Angrez* lines, entrenched on the Ridge. There were many sorties, and during the last one, only a few days before the city was stormed, our men performed great feats of valour, but they were repulsed and cut down to the last man. The Firangis lost many men, too, but the victory gave them great confidence. When their storming parties approached the walls and blew open the Kashmiri Gate, their leader Nikalsein, was seen waving his handkerchief on the point of his sabre from an elevated site. A ball struck him, and he fell. But his men forced their way through the city at the point of the bayonet, and Delhi is in Firangi hands again.'

'And what became of the King?' enquired Sarfaraz.

'He was made a prisoner, and his sons, who fled with him, were shot.'

'And so much for the rebellion,' said Sarfaraz Khan philosophically. "The city of Delhi was a garden of flowers, and now it is a ruined country; the stranger is not my enemy, nor is anyone my friend . . . ." '

'Don't grow sentimental and poetic, Sarfaraz,' said Javed Khan irritably. 'Who was it who came to my house to kill certain people?'

'It was I,' said Sarfaraz. 'But did I kill anyone?'

Behind the Curtain

It was now winter, though the cold winds had not yet begun to blow. Mother sold two of the silver spoons from the jewel box which she had rescued from our burning house, and used the money to make quilts and some warm clothing to keep away the cold.

Ever since we had heard of the fall of Delhi, a change had come over our outlook and our expectations. We began to look forward to the time when Shahjahanpur would be reoccupied by the British—it would mean the end of our captivity which, though it had been made pleasant by Kothiwali and Qamran and their households, was not a state to which we could resign ourselves forever; it would—we hoped—mean a reunion with other members of my mother's and father's families; and it would put an end to Javed Khan's plans to marry me. Our motives in hoping for the restoration of British authority were, therefore, entirely personal. We had, during the past months, come to understand much of the resentment against a foreign authority, and we saw that the continuation of that authority could only be an unhappy state of affairs for both sides; but for the time being, it was in our interests to see it restored. Our lives depended on it.

But as yet there was no sign of the approach of British soldiers. We had no doubt that they would arrive sooner or later, but of course we did not speak on the subject, nor did we consider it prudent to show too great an interest in what was happening elsewhere. Of Kothiwali's sympathy we were sure, but we were afraid lest Javed Khan, in his defeat and frustration, might try to inflict some injury on us.

One day the mohalla sweeperess, having taken ill, sent another girl to carry out her duties. The new girl recognized us as soon as she saw us, and a look of understanding passed between her and Mother. I remembered that she was called Mulia, and that she was the elder sister of a girl with whom I used to play when I was younger.

The latrine was the one place where we could manage any sort of privacy, and when Mulia went behind its curtain wall, Mother followed her.

'*Mausi,* you have no need to worry any more,' whispered Mulia. 'Delhi is taken, and your own people will be among us again. And I am to tell you that your brother is safe at Bharatpur. If you wish to send him a message, there is a person going on a pilgrimage to Mathura, and he will take your letter.'

Overjoyed at having met someone whom she knew and could trust, mother agreed to make use of the messenger.

'But what am I to write the letter with?' she asked.

'Don't worry,' said Mulia. 'Tomorrow I will bring paper and pencil. Meet me here again.'

We did not betray our feelings at this fortunate meeting, nor did anyone notice anything unusual about our behaviour. We did not even tell Anet or Granny about it, for fear that our hopes might be disappointed.

Next morning, keeping her promise, Mulia came again and waited for Mother behind the curtain wall. She handed her a scrap of paper and a small pencil, upon which Mother scribbled these words: 'I, Ruth, Anet, Mother, alive and well and hiding here. Do your best to take us away.'

She handed the note to Mulia, who slipped it into her bodice. Mulia then slipped away, leaving us in a state of suppressed excitement.

It was early January, and we had been with Kothiwali for over three months. We had wanted for nothing but had, on the contrary, been treated with great kindness and consideration. We were rather disappointed when it was suggested that we should return to Javed Khan's house. He came himself and asked Kothiwali to let us go. Perhaps he still hoped that Mother might be persuaded to give her consent to my marriage—months had passed since the British had taken Delhi, but there were still no signs of their arrival in Shahjahanpur.

Khan-Begum was not exactly overjoyed at our return, and was still subject to fits of jealousy. There must have been a heated argument between her and Javed, because the morning after our arrival we heard him exclaiming to her angrily: 'I hate this constant nagging of yours.' She gave him some reply, which was followed by the slash of Javed's whip and a long silence.

He left the house without speaking to anyone, and only came back in the evening for his dinner. He asked Khan-Begum if she had had anything to eat.

She replied: 'No, I am not hungry.'

'Then you had better sit down and eat,' he said, 'and don't put on any more of your airs.' She knew he was in a bad temper and had no wish to feel his whip again; so she did what he told her, though she remained glum and unfriendly until Kothiwali came and took us away again.

The Battle of Bichpuri

We were now in the middle of April 1858, and the hot winds of approaching summer brought the dust eddying into Kothiwali's veranda. The gulmohar tree outside the gate was aflame with scarlet flowers, and the mango trees were in blossom, promising fruit in abundance. The visits of Javed Khan to Kothiwali's house had of late become more frequent, and there were many whispered conversations between him and Kothiwali. We had no idea how we would fit in with their future plans should the British reoccupy Shahjahanpur.

One day Kothiwali received a visitor, a stranger whom we had not seen before. His name was Faizulla, and he too addressed Kothiwali as *chachi*, though he was not related to her. He was a brash young man, and gave a vivid account of his experiences at Fatehgarh, from where he had just returned.

'So you were present at the battle of Bichpuri?' asked Kothiwali.

'Yes, *chachi*,' he replied, 'and what a great battle it was! We fought the Firangis hand to hand, and made them feel the strength of our arms. I made a heap of the slain, and have brought with me a string of heads to present to the Nawab!'

'What a liar you are!' exclaimed Kothiwali.

'I swear by my head, *chachi*!'

'How did a thin fellow like you manage to carry so many heads?'

'Why, I slung them over my saddle, and rode home in triumph.'

'And who was it who got the worst of the fight?'

'Why, the kafirs, of course, *chachi*. We made a clean sweep of them,' and he passed the palm of his right hand over his left.

'Indeed!' said Kothiwali.

'There was not one man left, *chachi*, so do you know what they did? They sent their women out to fight us!'

'This becomes more intriguing,' said Kothiwali. 'You are a gifted boy, Faizulla—you have a wonderful imagination! Tell us, what did their women look like?'

'Well, they were rather big for women. Some of them wore false beards and mustachios. But every one of them had a high skirt with a metal disc hanging down in front.' (It suddenly dawned on me that Faizulla was describing a Scots regiment of Highlanders.) 'Such horrid looking women, I assure you. Of course, there was no question of fighting them. I don't lift my hands against women, and out of sheer disgust, I left the camp and came away.'

'You did right,' said Kothiwali. 'But will you not show us one of the Firangi heads you obtained?'

'I would be delighted to, *chachi*, but believe me, I have made a present of the whole string to the Nawab!'

Judging by the fact that Faizulla was safe at home instead of with a victorious army, we were fairly certain that they had been defeated by the British at Fatehgarh, and that it would not be long before Shahjahanpur was entered. This surmise was confirmed by Sarfaraz Khan who arrived at that moment and, giving Faizulla a look of scorn, said, 'So this warrior has been telling you of the Firangi heads he cut off ! Is he able to tell us who cut off Nizam Ali Khan's head?'

This announcement produced quite a sensation, and Kothiwali jumped up, exclaiming: 'Nizam Ali killed! You don't mean it!'

Nizam Ali Khan was probably the Nawab's most valued official, a moderate and widely respected man. We had once had the lease of his compound, and had always found him courteous and friendly.

'But I do mean it,' said Sarfaraz. 'I have it on better authority than the chatter of this bragging lout. There is mourning in Nizam Ali's family, and both his sons have been wounded—one in the head, the other in the leg.'

Faizulla, abashed at being found out, sat gazing at the ground while his hands, which had been busy with the slings of his rifle, now lay motionless.

'The Nawab sent out a strong force under Nizam Ali with instructions to prevent the Firangi army from crossing the Ganga. But they were too slow and cumbrous, and the enemy had made two marches towards our city before Nizam Ali sighted them. The Firangi troops had just reached their camping ground when they noticed a cloud of dust rising on the horizon. Their scouts brought them the intelligence that the Nawab's army was marching upon them, and the cavalry was immediately ordered to remount and prepare for action. They attacked the Nawabi force before the latter had time to form, while the light guns raked them in the flank. Taken by surprise, our soldiers were demoralized. They were seized by panic, and broke and fled.'

'And what about Nizam Ali?' asked Kothiwali impatiently.

'He made a desperate attempt to keep his men together and to put up some sort of resistance, but his efforts were in vain. He could not bring any of his men together to make a stand. His gunners could not fire, as the fugitive soldiers surged from one part of the field to the other. Resolved not to survive this disgrace, Nizam Ali dismounted, and requested his servant to pass his sword through his body. But the servant would not. Then Nizam Ali rushed about madly and put his head into the mouth of a cannon, and ordered a gunner to apply a match and blow him to pieces. But the gunner refused. Poor Nizam Ali! He was about to stab himself with his poignard when the Firangi cavalry came thundering down like a torrent, sweeping all before them. A *sawar* belonging to De Kantzow's Horse recognized him— Nizam Ali's distinctive appearance could not be mistaken—and wheeling round, charged him at full gallop and pinned him with his lance to the ground. And so ended the life of a man who possessed more determination and character than Abdul Rauf Khan, and who was the mainstay of the Nawabi. With Nizam Ali gone, I doubt if the Nawab's government will last another week.'

'I am truly sorry to hear of his fate,' said Kothiwali with a sigh. 'But what became of his sons? You said that two of them were wounded.'

'Better that they had been killed by the side of their noble father. Why, they joined in the stampede and fled from the field of battle as fast as their horses could carry them, following the example of my friend Faizulla here. I have just left them beating their heads and yelling like old women over their fallen fortunes.'

'You are the bearer of serious news,' said Kothiwali. 'Unless I am very much mistaken, the Firangi army will soon be here. What will become of us, then?'

'They are marching this way, that is certain,' said Sarfaraz. 'There can be no doubt that the city will soon be reoccupied. We must think of how to save ourselves, because it is certain that they will order the city to be sacked, as was done at Delhi. It has become the custom now.'

'Allah forbid!' cried Kothiwali. 'Let us all meet this evening at my house and discuss measures for our safety. No time must be lost, because tomorrow the Firangi army is sure to be in the district, and the day after they will enter the city.'

And so, Kothiwali, who had remained quietly at home all through the most violent stages of the revolt, now showed her qualities as a leader. She ordered these rough, disorderly men about as though they were children, and brought about a sense of organization, where otherwise, panic might have prevailed.

In Flight Again

That evening Kothiwali said to Mother, 'Well Mariam, the Firangis are coming. I am glad that you are with me. Should it be necessary for us to flee the city, you will come with us, won't you?'

'Yes,' said Mother, 'for how will they know us for what we are? We have no one among them who would receive and protect us. From our complexions and our clothes they would take us for Mohammedan women, and we will receive the same treatment as your women. No, for the present we are identified with you all, and we must go where you go.'

When it was decided by Kothiwali that she and her family should flee Shahjahanpur, it was agreed by everyone that the rendezvous would be Javed Khan's house. We left for his house that same evening. There was Kothiwali's family; Qamran's family; and a doctor and his family, whom we had never seen before. Including Javed and his family, there were about thirty persons gathered at his house that evening, the 28th of April, 1858. It was almost a year since we had left our own burning house behind. Before long, Javed Khan's house would be burning too. It did not make any sense at all; but I suppose war never has made sense to ordinary individuals.

There was of course, no sleeping that night, for *meana* after *meana* kept dropping in till late, and there were whispers and secret consultations. The decision arrived at was that we should make our flight in a northerly direction, as the British force was marching from the south. And so, early on the morning of the 29th, long before dawn, the *meanas* began to fill up.

We had expected to get a seat in one of the *meanas* but soon they were all full and there was no room left.

Javed Khan came up to us and said, 'Mariam, you had better get into the doctor's bullock-cart. You will be quite comfortable there.'

There was no other choice; and so the four of us—Granny, Mother, Anet and myself—took our seats in the cart. Beside us was the doctor's wife, and her brothers' wives, and their children. The party set off at once, the men riding ahead on their horses, while the *meana*-bearers trotted along at a brisk pace, and our bullock-cart trundled along in the rear.

After about two hours we reached the village of Indarkha, some eight miles out of Shahjahanpur. The sun was up, and when we raised the cloth which formed the roof of our cart, we were astonished to find ourselves alone, for the *meanas* and horsemen had all disappeared. It seemed that our driver had taken a circuitous route, and we had been left well behind. And there we were, in a strange village, and with companions who were unknown to us.

The doctor enquired for a vacant house where we could rest, but there was none to be had. The villagers were quite indifferent to our plight, and told us that we could not put up in the village. But the doctor grew bold, and brought them round to the notion that it was their duty to accomodate us all, whoever we were. Finally they told him: 'There really is no vacant house in the village, but there is one thing you can do. At the southern end of the village, just opposite the big banyan tree, a new house is being built. It is not yet complete, but it is habitable. You may occupy it and remain in it for a short time.' And so we gladly got down from our cart and entered a mud structure which consisted of a line of rooms at one end, a courtyard in front, and a wall all round.

We were, in a way, the guests of the doctor and his wife, and they were very kind to us. He was a Bengali Muslim, and had belonged to the Shahjahanpur regiment, but had severed his connection with it when it had marched out to Bareilly on the 1st of June, 1857. Renting a house in the city, he soon acquired a reputation for possessing a healing hand and his practice flourished.

The doctor's sisters-in-law now busied themselves with digging and setting up an oven. One of them lighted it and set a pot of dal on the fire, while the other kneaded flour and began to make chapattis.

That evening, after everyone had eaten, the doctor came in and sat down, and in very civil language asked Mother to tell him who she was and what her cirumstances were. Mother told him our story, which aroused his sympathy and compassion.

'Do you think,' asked Mother, 'do you think that British authority will be restored again?'

'I do not know about the distant future,' he replied, 'but certainly their authority will be restored. But, I was going to say that now you are with us, I hope you will make yourself at home and command me in any way you please. We are all in the same boat at present, so let us help each other as best we can.'

Mother was touched by his expression of goodwill, and we remained with him that night and the next day. Long after sunset, when everything was still and the noisy birds in the banyan tree were silent, the doctor came to Mother and said, 'Javed Khan has come and he wants to speak to you.'

'Why has he come?' asked Mother. 'What further business has he with us?'

'He seems most anxious to see you,' said the doctor. 'He cannot come in here, but you can speak to him at the door.'

Mother went out to meet Javed Khan and I, being curious, followed her and stood in the shadow of the wall.

'Mariam,' said Javed, 'I have come to say that the Firangis have reoccupied Shahjahanpur. You will not, of course, go to them, but don't forget the protection you have received from me.'

'I will not forget it,' said mother. 'I am grateful to you for giving us shelter. And I will never forget the kindness shown to me by Kothiwali and Qamran.'

'I have only one request to make,' said Javed, uneasily shifting his weight from one foot to the other.

'Yes, what is it?' asked Mother.

'I know that the time has passed when I could speak of marrying your daughter,' he said. 'It is too late now to do anything about that.

But will you permit me to see her once more, before I leave?'

'What good will that do?' began mother; but impelled by some odd impulse, I stepped forward into the light and stood before Javed Khan.

He gazed at me in silence for about a minute, and for the first time I did not take my eyes away from his; then, without a smile or a word, he turned away and mounted his horse and rode away into the night.

The Final Journey

The doctor spoke to Mother the next morning: 'I have heard that yesterday the British army entered Shahjahanpur and that a civil government has already been established. Won't you go to them now that order has been restored?'

'A good suggestion,' said Mother, 'but who will we know among them?'

The doctor said, 'You will be known at once by your voice, your accent and your manner, and perhaps you will find that some of your own relatives have arrived and are looking for you.'

The doctor then went to the village elders and told them that mother was a European lady who had escaped during the massacre, and that she and her family wished to go into Shahjahanpur. Now that civil authority had been restored, would anyone undertake to carry them into town on his cart?

'You are not telling us anything we don't know,' said the headman. 'As soon as they stepped down from your bullock-cart we knew who they were.'

'How did you know?' asked the doctor.

'You must take me for a pumpkin,' said the old man. 'Why, their very walk and their carriage indicated who they were. I marked their legs particularly. Those are not the feet, thought I, of women who go about barefooted. The way they treaded gingerly on the hot sand was proof enough. So they want to return to Shahjahanpur, do they? Well I, Gangaram, shall take them in my own cart, and will reach them to any spot in Shahjahanpur where they wish to go. Tomorrow, in the morning, I shall be ready.'

We put our few belongings together and the next day, at about ten, we got into Gangaram's bullock-cart and set out for Shahjahanpur.

Our journey was uneventful. We reached the town late in the afternoon, and asked Gangaram to take us to our old house, for we did not know where else we could go. As we halted before the ruins of our old house, Mr Redman came up and told Mother briefly of his own escape and his family's. He informed us that the British Commander-in-Chief had reoccupied the district, but had since then continued his march to Bareilly, leaving a small force under Colonel Hall to guard Shahjahanpur. He said the town was not quite safe yet, as the Maulvi of Faizabad was still in control of the eastern boundary of the district; and he advised us to take shelter in the quarters he was occupying with his family. Mother was reluctant to accept his invitation, but we were still homeless and without any male protection, and so we stopped for the night in the building in which the Redmans had taken shelter. Here we met a party of three men whom my uncle had sent from Bharatpur to escort us to him. One was a mounted orderly named Nasim Khan, and the other two were servants of the Maharaja of Bharatpur. We came to know that the note sent through Mulia had actually been delivered to my uncle, and he took immediate steps for our rescue. Mother wept to see the familiar handwriting of her brother, and to read his letter which was full of affection and anxiety for our welfare, and contained a pressing invitation to come to him at Bharatpur where, he said, she would find a home for the rest of her life.

This was on Sunday, the 3rd of May 1858. Next morning we were surprised to see Pilloo's mother arrive in our midst—without Pilloo! She looked so upset that we felt certain Pilloo had been killed; but when at last we got her to speak coherently, we discovered that Pilloo had decided to remain behind of his own accord! He had grown so attached to Mangal Khan that he refused to come away, and his mother had to leave without him, hoping he would relent and follow her. But he never did: he preferred the companionship of the Pathan, and continued to live with him and his family. We never did understand his behaviour.

While we were listening to Pilloo's mother's tale of woe, Mr Redman returned from a visit to Colonel Hall's camp, and invited us all to sit down to breakfast. We had, however, scarcely eaten anything, when an alarm was raised that the rebel army, under the Maulvi of Faizabad, was crossing the Khannaut by the bridge of boats. Nasim Khan, my uncle's man, who had gone to bathe his horse at the river, came running back at the same time, with the report that the enemy had driven in the vedettes of the little force led by the Colonel, who had entrenched himself in the Old Jail. There was a smell of battle in the air. The sound of bugles, the neighing of horses, the clatter of riderless mounts dashing across the plain, the dull thump of guns, and the confused noise of men running in different directions; all these were unmistakable signs that a considerable force had attacked the small British garrison.

We had no time to lose if we were to save ourselves. Gangaram's cart was still at our disposal. Though Mr Redman assured Mother that there was no danger, she was determined to make for the countryside where she thought we would be safer. We all climbed into the cart: Granny, Mother, myself, Anet, Pilloo's mother, and Vicky, the Redman's daughter. We were scarcely out of the compound gate when we heard shouts, and, amidst a cloud of dust, some ten or twelve troopers of the rebel cavalry came riding at full gallop, flourishing their sabres in the air, and surrounded our cart. We heard one of them say: 'Here are some of them, let us finish them off!' We expected that at any moment they would tear the covering from over our heads and bury their shining blades in our bosoms. Little Vicky held her neck with both her hands, saying: 'Let us all put our hands round our necks so that only our fingers will be cut off and our heads will be safe!'

Everyone was unnerved except for Mother. With her eyes almost starting out of their sockets, her face haggard and lined after months of sorrow and uncertainty, she grasped the handle of her knife, while with her free hand, she removed the covering and put out her head. Her expression was enough to frighten even these ruffians who were thirsting for our blood. They reined back.

'What do you want with us, young fellows?' said Mother. 'Is there anything unusual about seeing so many helpless females fleeing from the city to escape dishonour and death?'

They did not stop to hear any more. Believing us to be Muslim women escaping from the city, they turned about and tackled Nasim Khan, who was riding behind us. But he had the presence of mind to tell them that he was a soldier of the faith, and that the women in the cart were his relatives, leaving the city as the Firangis had occupied it.

After the troopers had gone, Gangaram came down from the cart, and folding his hands before Mother, exclaimed: 'Well done! You are weak in body, but you have the spirit of a goddess! I do not know of any other woman who could have dealt so well with those men.'

Our adventures did not end there. Scarcely had we started moving again when, with a heavy thud, the cart fell down on its side. The axle had broken. There was no possibility of repairing it on the spot. We had to push on somehow, if we did not wish to fall in with another detachment of the enemy. The whirring and crashing of shells, the rattle of musketry, and the shouts of soldiers could be distinctly heard. We got down from the cart and, bidding goodbye to Gangaram, began to walk. We had no idea where we were walking, but it was our intention to get as far away as possible from the fighting.

After an hour of walking under the hot sun, we met a number of baggage carts passing along the highway. They belonged to the British army and were going, like ourselves, in the direction of Bareilly. One of the Sikh escorts saw us, and took pity on our condition. Mother had a high fever, and kept asking to be left alone by the wayside while we went on and found a place of safety. Nasim Khan dismounted and put her up on his horse, while he walked alongside, supporting Mother with his hands. At this moment another accident took place.

As Nasim Khan was dismounting, his pistol went off. This threw us all into a panic once more.

Nasim Khan looked puzzled and turned round several times before he realized what had happened. 'Oh, how stupid of me!' he exclaimed. 'I had cocked it when we met the maulvi's men. But, as usual, it goes off only when the enemy is out of sight!'

The Sikh soldiers burst into laughter, and we could not help joining in, though our own laughter was rather hysterical. Then the Sikhs offered us a lift in one of the baggage carts, and Anet, Vicky and I gratefully accepted it, for we were completely tired out.

We journeyed on like this for another three or four miles until we reached a small village where we were offered shelter. As it was now afternoon, and there was no shelter in the baggage cart from the blazing sun, we were only too glad to accept the villagers' hospitality.

Two days later, having hired a cart, we proceeded towards the south and, avoiding the main highways, reached Fatehgarh after four days. There we joined up with Mr Redman's party; and Mother called on the Collector, who gave her some 'succour-money', which enabled us to continue our journey to Bharatpur in comparative comfort.

Ten days later we were in the home of my uncle, where we found rest, shelter and comfort, until a rumour that a rebel force was about to cross the territory threw us all into a panic again. It was only a rumour. But the trials of the past year had made such an impression on my mind, that I was often to wake up terrified from nightmares in which I saw again those fierce swordsmen running through the little church, slashing at anyone who came in their way. However, our troubles were really over when we arrived at Bharatpur, and we settled down to a quiet and orderly life, though it was never to be the same again without my father.

We did not hear again of Lala Ramjimal and his family. We would have liked to thank him for his kindness to us, and for risking his own life in protecting us; but beyond the knowledge that he had settled with his family in Bareilly, we received no further news of him.

We heard that Kothiwali and Qamran and their families eventually returned to Shahjahanpur, after life had returned to normal. But Javed Khan disappeared and was never seen again. Perhaps he had escaped into Nepal. It is more probable that he was caught and hanged with some other rebels. Secretly, I have always hoped that he succeeded in escaping. Looking back on those months when we were his prisoners, I cannot help feeling a sneaking admiration for him. He was very wild and muddle-headed, and often cruel, but he was also very handsome and gallant, and there was in him a streak of nobility which he did his best to conceal. But perhaps I really admire him, because he thought I was beautiful.

Notes

Pathans formed thirty per cent of the Muslim population of Shahjahanpur (Muslims forming twenty-three per cent of the entire population) according to the 1901 census. Most were cultivators, although many were landed proprietors of the district. (True Pathans are descendants of Afghan immigrants.) 'Their attitude during the Mutiny cost them dear, as many estates were forfeited for rebellion'. (*Gazetteer*)

Most of the rebel leaders were either killed or brought to trial, and in all cases their property was confiscated. Ghulam Qadir Khan died shortly after the reoccupation and his estates were seized.

The number of Muslims whose services (to the British) were recognized was extremely small, as, apart from the two men who sheltered their European kinsman, Mr Maclean, in pargana Tilhar, the only persons recognized were Nasir Khan and Amir Ali of Shahjahanpur, who buried the bodies of the Englishmen murdered on the occasion of the outbreak, and Ghulam Husain, who saved the commissariat buildings from destruction and for some time protected several Hindus on the district staff. (p. 150, *Gazetteer*, 1900)

At Jalalabad, the tehsildar Ahmed Yar Khan at once showed his sympathy with the rebels by releasing several criminals under arrest. On the arrival of Ghulam Qadir at Shahjahanpur, the tehsildar was raised to the dignity of *nezim*, but his tyranny aroused the resistance of the Rajputs of Khandar and other villages. (p. 248, *Gazetteer*)

'Mr Lemaistre, a clerk in the Collector's office, was killed in the church, and the fate of his daughter is unknown.'

(*The Meerut Mofussilite*, 1858)

The city was populated by a large body of Afghans sent there by Bahadur Khan (a soldier of fortune in the service of Jehangir and later Shahjahan), at that time serving beyond the Indus. The story goes that these Afghans belonged to 52 tribes and that each had its own mohalla, many quarters of the city to this day being named after Pathan clans. . . . The history of the town and of Bahadur Khan's family is told in an anonymous work called the *Shahjahanpurnama* or the *Anhar-ul-bahr,* written in 1839, and also in the *Akbar-i-Muhabbat* of Nawab Muhabbat Khan.

I first heard the story of Mariam and her daughter from my father, who was born in the Shahjahanpur military cantonment a few years after the Mutiny. That, and my interest in the accounts of those who had survived the 1857 uprising, took me to Shahjahanpur on a brief visit in the late 1960s. It was one of those small U.P. towns that had resisted change, and there were no high-rise buildings or blocks of flats to stifle the atmosphere. I found the old church of St Mary's without any difficulty, and beside it a memorial to those who were killed there on that fateful day. It was surrounded by a large, open parade ground, bordered by mango groves and a few old bungalows. It couldn't have been very different in Ruth Labadoor's time. The little River Khannaut was still crossed by a bridge of boats.